THE TIME BORROWER

Also by this author:

The Face Out of Time

Ripple Rider: An Anguillan Adventure in Time

The Last Tag

The Light Rider Series:

Light Riders and the Morenci Mine Murder

Light Riders and the Fleur-de-lis Murder

Light Riders and the Missouri Mud Murder

The Time Borrower

(A *Light Rider's* Novel)

A Time Travel Mystery by
Ann I. Goldfarb

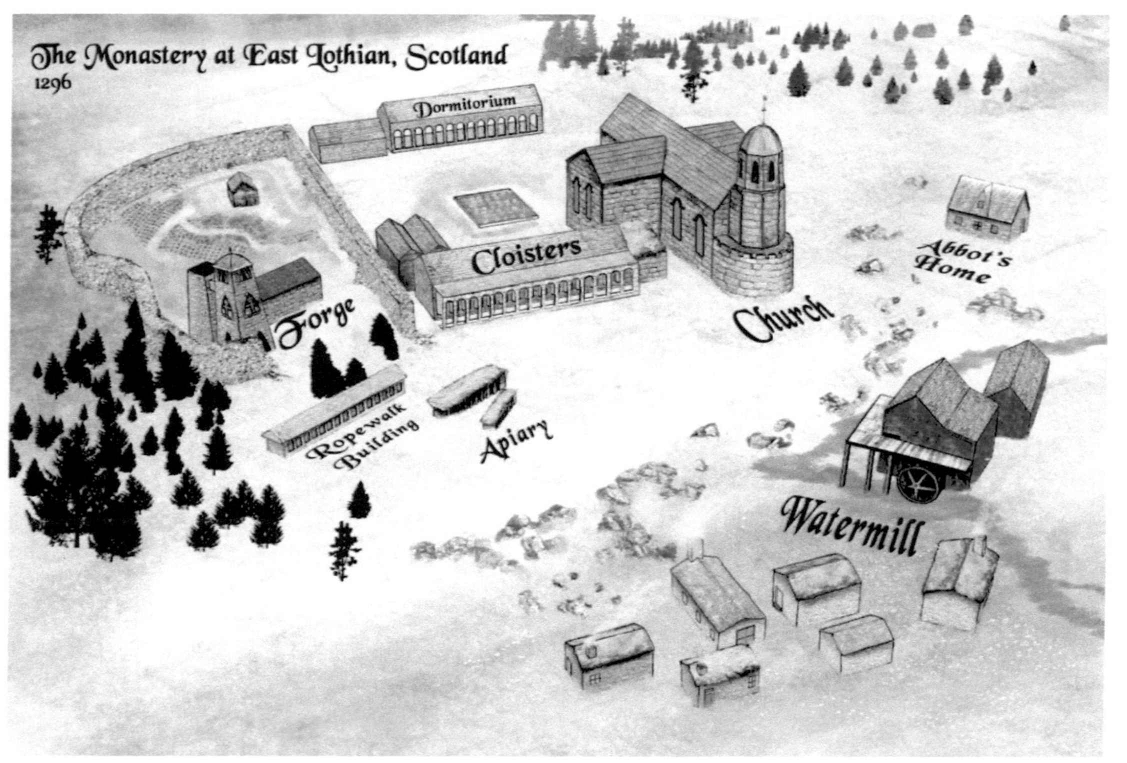

The Monastery at East Lothian, Scotland
1296
Dormitorium
Cloisters
Forge
Church
Abbot's Home
Ropewalk Building
Apiary
Watermill

The Monks of the Abbey
in East Lothian, Scotland, 1296

Brother Alban, The Precentor
Brother Jarvin
Brother Trewyn
Brother Rulf, the red-haired conversi monk
Brother Gregory, the green-eyed scribe

The Monastery Structure

The Abbot – Head of the monastery

The Sacrist – Head of maintenance for the church and its sacred items

The Precentor – Facilitator of the worship service

The Prior – The abbot's assistant or deputy

The Kitchener – Monk in charge of the kitchen

The Cellarer – Head of household for general provisions

The Infirmarian – Monk in charge of caring for the sick

The Almoner – Monk in charge of distributing alms (food, money, provisions) to the poor

The Fraterer – Monk in charge of the linens and dining set-up

The Roundsman – Monk in charge of the general welfare of the abbey and its buildings

Lay Brothers – Workers in the abbey who tended the animals and did the farming, also includes the masons and construction workers

Conversi – Monks who did not enter the abbey as children, but rather, those who were the workers and farmers

Part One:
Dead Monks

Chapter One:
Ryn, Boston, MA,
Present Day

"Stop crying Linna. I can't understand a word you're saying. This is a lousy phone connection."

"I said 'someone's about to be killed.' Oh my God, Ryn!"

"Call the police! Hang up and dial 911!"

"It won't help. This is awful."

"What do you mean it won't help? Sobbing to me certainly isn't going to save whoever's getting killed. You want me to call 911 for you?"

"No. He's already dead. Or he will be."

"Linna, who's dead? Who's going to be dead?"

"I don't know his name."

"Where are you calling from?"

"My apartment in Georgetown."

"And you're watching an attempted murder?"

"No, not exactly."

"Then what? What exactly? How do you know someone's getting killed?"

"Because I read what he wrote."

"Huh?"

"This guy, he's a monk. A monk who lived in the 13th century, and someone's going to kill him."

"The 13th century? Like 1200 A.D.? You're hysterical over someone who died in the 13th century? What the hell, Linna! I'm in the middle of finals!"

"And I'm in the middle of translating some liturgies from an old monastery in Scotland. Part of my internship this summer. And that's when I figured it out, Ryn. The liturgy. It was encrypted. Whoever wrote the verses hid the message. But someone's going to kill him."

"I hate to break it to you, Linna, but it's what? Eight centuries later? The guy is already dead!"

I could feel my neck getting red. All I wanted to do was hit "end" and finish the call. Just like Linna had done to our relationship at the end of high school. *"I think it's time we start to see other people, Ryn. After all, we'll both be at different colleges next year."* Click. *Well, "click" to you, too, Linna.* But I couldn't do that to her. Even two years later, I still had it bad for Linna Sullivan. I took a deep breath and continued.

"Why are you calling me? We haven't talked in years." *And I should have changed my phone number.*

"Because you're the only one who can help me. Help him, actually. The poor monk who wrote the messages."

"And how exactly am I going to do that?"

Linna had stopped crying and her voice dropped to barely a whisper.

"You know how. Don't think I didn't realize what you and your sister could do with time."

"My sister? Did Aeden put you up to this?"

"Of course not. I haven't spoken to her since graduation. Look, all I'm asking is that you show me how to borrow time. I'll wind up figuring it out for myself eventually. But this doomed monk … I've got to do something."

I kept my mouth shut and let Linna go on.

"I took a chance calling you, Ryn. I wasn't even sure you'd talk to me. In fact, I wasn't even sure you kept the same number and ..."

Damn. I knew I should have changed my phone number. I let out a slow breath as Linna finished her sentence.

"I don't know how to explain it, but I feel so drawn to that monk, so compelled to …"

"To what? Save him? Because if that's what you're thinking, you can forget it. Hey, it was nice talking to you, Linna. Good luck with your internship."

"WAIT! Don't hang up. Please don't hang up. I'll be back home in Portland for a few days next week. Will you at least see me when your finals are over?"

"I'm not going back to Portland. I've got a summer job in Boston."

"Then I'll fly there first and meet you. Even if it's just for an hour or so."

"This monk? This murder thing. It's that important to you?"

"Yes. It really is."

I paused long enough for Linna to ask again.

"So is it okay? Will you see me?"

"I suppose I could spare an hour."

And that's how it started. I let an ex-girlfriend back into my life, and with it, something even worse.

Chapter Two:
Linna

It wasn't as if I set out to call Ryn in the first place. I mean, we hadn't talked in years, and we didn't exactly part on the friendliest of terms. There's no handbook or basic operational guidelines for breaking up with your boyfriend. I just didn't want to have "any strings attached" when we started college that fall. But Ryn didn't see it that way. So when desperation forced me to call him two years later, I wasn't surprised that he was still angry.

Not many interns get the chance to translate original medieval writing like the 13th-century roll of parchment that was entrusted to my care. But…it held a deadly secret. And Ryn was the only person who could help me.

I didn't notice it at first. I was too focused on translating each separate word and then piecing them together. The cursive, if you could call it that, made it even more difficult. It was only when I took my eyes away from the parchment and glanced back that I caught it. Like one of those letter puzzles people are always posting on Facebook. What's the first word that you see? Love? Money? Dreams? Only what I saw ran like a thread, weaving in front of my eyes. Hadn't anyone noticed this before? I mean, it wasn't something you could easily dismiss.

And then I realized—this is probably the first time the liturgy was being translated. It was a lesser-known work that came to the university with a number of highly prized and valuable texts. All of them were stored in an underground vault in the monastery for centuries until the museum and the colleges received that grant.

It was personal. The coded messages. I felt as if I had opened someone's diary without permission. But the more I read, the more I had to read. I was working so late in the classics library that security had to escort me out of the building, insisting that I call a cab and not walk to my apartment.

I guess if it were just a single piece of parchment, I could have just translated it and let it go. But as it turned out, the university had received a number of codices, or bound books, and a few ancient scrolls, including the one that was given to me for translation. These works were so detailed, so intense; it was no wonder scholars spent decades studying them. Like them, I had perfected a skill that was virtually useless in the 21st century. That is, up until now. I knew how to analyze and read medieval writing. There's actually a word for it—paleography. But when you mention it to someone, they look at you as if you're talking astrology or soothsaying. Not much of a market for transcribing old liturgies. Unless you wind up at some academic institution where someone, for some reason, bestowed an obscene amount of money for that purpose.

They must have been expecting the usual stuff—written Scripture that listed the order of the prayers, or perhaps a special order for reading psalms. And essentially, this is what it was. With one exception—the formula for murder. It was spelled out. Step by step. That monk knew what was happening. Then why didn't he go to the abbot? He had evidence. He could have saved himself. Why did he choose not to? Unless...his murder was just a small part of some tangled web. Something so heinous and so vile that to uncover it would have destroyed the very foundation of the monastery.

My mind conjured up all sorts of images. But worst of all, I started to see the face of that monk every night when I closed my eyes. Straight dark hair that tumbled over his forehead. Bold brown eyes and a subtle smile. I was becoming obsessed. And that's when I knew I had to change the course of events, even if it meant pleading with an ex-boyfriend.

Chapter Three:
Ryn

I couldn't believe I was actually jealous of some monk who died centuries ago, but I was. Jealous and pissed off. It took me a full year to get over Linna and now with one phone call, it's like she just dumped me again. Damn it! And like an idiot, I agreed to meet her. A quick ten-minute conversation and I'd be on my way. I wasn't about to get involved with her and I sure as hell wasn't about to mess around with time travel again. Besides, Aeden and I never got those formulas totally right anyway. And, I had a decent summer job in the bioengineering lab, even if it was just as an assistant to the assistant lab tech.

Linna and I agreed to meet at the Starbucks in the lobby of her hotel on Copley Square. She was already sitting at a table, latte in hand, when I arrived. Her straight black hair was shorter, and it looked as if she hadn't had a good night's sleep in days, but still, Linna was hot. Before I could say anything, she spoke.

"Thanks, Ryn, for seeing me. I was beginning to think you'd bail out."

"You took an extra flight before heading to Portland, so I wasn't going to stand you up."

"I'll make it brief. I just want to borrow your formulas. I don't know how else to explain it, but ever since I figured out what was going on in the monastery, I knew I had to do something. That sweet, gentle man with the heart of a poet is going to be killed. And I…I…"

I saw the look in her eye and all but freaked out.

"Oh my God, Linna! You're in love with this guy! This monk. No, let me be clear. This already, eight centuries later, DEAD monk! I don't know what's worse. The dead part or the monk part!"

"It's not what you think."

"Oh no? Then what is it? Tell me, because I'm not your time travel agent."

I could see Linna's eyes getting wet, and I heard her sniffle.

"Don't start crying. If I wanted to watch someone cry, I'd go see one of my sister's theater performances. Look, I get it. You wanted to meet other guys. But for God sake, Linna, I didn't expect you to dredge them up from the DEAD ZONE."

She swallowed and looked directly at me.

"You wanted to know. Here goes. When I first started translating the liturgies, it was just a puzzle. Coded text. Secret messages. And I felt so smug. I was the only one who had seen them. But as I continued, it became more than that. This monk let me into his world. And I began to see the things he did. To revel in the soft beauty of the dawn or to brush aside the last of the winter's snow to reveal a tiny bud …."

"Pull yourself together, Linna. You're sounding worse than those sappy lines in one of Aeden's stupid romantic plays. I think you've lost it! You need to put aside those liturgies or whatever they are and get back into the real world."

"I knew you wouldn't understand. But this monk is such a gentle soul. And just knowing that someone is going to snuff the life out of him is more than I can handle."

"Then ask your advisor to give you something else to translate. Something boring and uneventful."

"That's not funny, Ryn. It's too late. I know too much. And I need to act. I just hoped you'd save me some time by giving me the complete formulas for bending light."

"Bending light? How did you…"

"I wasn't trying to snoop. But a few years ago, right before our final in physics, we were studying in your room. You went down the hall to get us a snack, and I sort of rummaged around the papers that were on your desk. That's when I saw the formulas. Snell's Law. Other stuff, too. Things that weren't part of our curriculum. Side notes about time, space and dimensionality. I made myself a copy and tucked it away. I didn't take a second look until recently. And that's when it started to make sense."

"What did?"

"The fact that you and your sister seemed to know things that weren't readily available in textbooks. You had firsthand knowledge. So don't lie to me. If I wanted to go viral with this, I would have done so a long time ago. So was I right? You used light to time travel?"

"Stay put, Linna. I need to get a cup of coffee."

As I stood up and walked to the counter, I watched her bite her lip and look down. Linna was one of the smartest girls in our graduating class. Full scholarships to Ivy League schools and more awards than the rest of us put together. So, yeah. She was right. She'd probably figure out the formulas without my help. But the formulas weren't perfect. Something always went wrong, and that could happen to her, too.

For such a smart girl, you're really screwed up, Linna Sullivan.

Chapter Four:
Linna

As he faced the counter, I could see that Ryn had gotten taller over the past two years and his shoulders seemed broader. For an instant, a vision flashed across my brain of him climbing or rappelling down some sort of cliff or building, using only his hands and the tips of his feet. The image flashed in front of me, and then it faded as if it were the remnants of an early morning dream. Sleep deprivation will do that to you. I took a quick sip of my latte and watched as he ordered his coffee. He was still the Ryn I remembered, the team player who excelled at soccer, lacrosse, and swimming. But there was something else, something I couldn't place. I glanced down at the papers in front of me as he returned to our table and spoke.

"It was a long time ago, Linna. I was only thirteen and Aeden was twelve. We got stuck cleaning out this hoarder's nest that belonged to a great aunt of ours in Waddell, Arizona. She was some sort of scientist, and as if hoarding pieces of crap from here to Timbuktu wasn't enough, she found a way to use light for time travel. Aeden and I messed around with it and got stuck in the 1930s. Freakin' ugly mess. We swore we'd never do it again. But we did. Two more times. And there's no control. Not really. Other things play into the time-space continuum and screw you up."

"But you did it. You time traveled."

I nodded.

"I need to do this, Ryn. I need to help this guy. I will never be able to live with myself if I don't."

"Linna, if you think you're going to change history, think again. One seemingly insignificant thing, like picking flowers or humming a tune, can have endless repercussions. And if you really set out to change something, like prevent a murder, then the reper-cussions may be monumental."

"I'm not looking to change the world, Ryn. Just to allow someone kind and gentle to live in it for the rest of his natural life."

"You're as obtuse as my sister. Don't you get it? That *is* changing the world. And by the way, I am really pissed that you went through the stuff on my desk that day."

"But I never told anyone. And I wouldn't tell anyone now. So will you help me or not? My flight for Portland leaves in three hours, and I have to check out of the hotel and get to the airport."

"You do realize that even if you time travel, it will only take you back in time, not place. So if this monastery is in Scotland, you'd be in Portland, right around the time the Anasazi people were building their kivas in the Southwest. And honestly, I don't know if anyone was building anything near Portland in the 1200s. Just you and a hell of a lot of land. Good luck with that, Linna."

"But that's where you're wrong, Ryn. You only know the light part. Snell's part. Un-refracted light can be bent to move you back in time, but it's the vibration that hones in on the relative dimensionality in space. Natural frequencies, when combined with refracted light, should be able to compensate for actual distance."

"Well, thank you, Doctor Who, for the insight. And how exactly do you intend to prove this?"

"The only way I know how. To conceal my identity and travel back eight centuries to Lothian, Scotland."

"This isn't a freakin' ride in Disneyworld. I can't even begin to tell you how dangerous it is. And besides, how are you even going to communicate with anyone? You won't understand a word of the Scottish language. Hell, we could barely figure out the stories from *Canterbury Tales* in our junior year, and that was *with* the lousy translation!"

"But I understand Latin, and that's the language they were using in the monasteries."

"News flash, Linna! They didn't exactly set out the welcome mats for women!"

"I can always go incognito. Anyway, all of this is moot unless you help me out. I have the formulas. I've spent hours figuring out how the vibrations work, but the thing I'm missing…is what you figured out a long time ago. The angles. The geometry of it all. Without the correct angles emanating from a light source, I wouldn't be able to calculate distance back in time. So will you do it? Explain how the angles work?"

Ryn tapped his knuckles on the table and stood up.

"I need another cup of coffee."

I reached over and grabbed his arm.

"I'll never ask you for anything again. Just this."

"Well, at least you've got that right. Grab a piece of paper or a napkin. I haven't got all day."

Chapter Five:
Ryn

Linna and I finished our conversation in less than an hour. I left Starbucks knowing she'd get on her plane and that would be it. No more Linna Sullivan for another few years if I was lucky. *Go track down your mystery monk. Have a great life.* I had tried to reason with her before I left, but I knew it was useless.

"You're making a mistake, Linna. Are you familiar with the word *reckless*? Because it's a freaking understatement for what you're about to do. And no one can help you once it's done."

"You think I don't know that? You think this is just some stupid whim? Well, it's not. It's …"

"Save your breath. You're going to need it."

"Ryn! Just one more thing and I'll say good-bye. I need to know. What does it feel like? This time travel thing?"

"Like the worst centrifugal force amusement ride you've ever taken. Only in the dark, with no air. Think of it as having an asthma attack underwater. *Fortunatos, Linna.* Guess I must remember some Latin after all."

I was just about to the door when I realized something. Something that forced me to go back. As I turned towards her table she had already stood up and was heading towards me.

"Ryn, I…"

"Before you say anything, I need to ask you something. How on earth are you going to figure out the right year? I mean, do you even know the year? That monk could have lived at any time during the 13th century."

"1296."

"What?"

"1296. That was the year. And the month was May. I need to reach that monastery by April of 1296 or it will be too late."

"How can you be so sure?"

"Because the monk encrypted the date as well. You know the Roman numerals as well as I do, that part wasn't hard to figure out. And with the formulas for light and vibration, I can be there."

At this point Linna was standing so close to me that I could smell the cinnamon latte on her breath. I reached my hand and grabbed her wrist, leaning in so that none of the customers could hear us.

"I'm telling you again, Linna, this is wrong. This is the worst possible thing you could do."

"You're still angry with me, aren't you?"

"This has nothing to do with that."

I let go of her wrist, but she didn't move.

"It'll be okay, Ryn. I just need to do this."

"Whatever. It's your life."

I wanted to leave quickly, in case she decided to cry. Instead, I looked right at her and shook my head.

"It's always cold in Scotland."

Then, I hightailed it for the door and didn't look back.

*****

As I ran to catch the bus to campus, I couldn't help but think about my sister, Aeden, and her reaction if she found out that there was actually a way to use vibration as a means to compensate for space and dimensionality. I knew her so well that I could almost hear the conversation

"Ryn! Do you know what that means? Do you have any idea? We could actually go back to the early 1600s and watch a Shakespearean play at the Globe Theatre in London! Or sit on the slopes of the Acropolis for a Greek tragedy in Athens! Oh my gosh. Imagine. Sitting in the Theater of Dionysus!"

Yep, there was no way I was telling Aeden about this. It was bad enough having to read that stuff in high school, let alone sit through it! After that last fiasco of ours, I made a promise to her that we wouldn't time travel again, and I intended to keep my word.

And Aeden was back in Portland now. Her school term at Emerson College ended last week. Just as well.

If she even had a hint of what we could do, my life would become unbearable.

"Leave well enough alone" certainly applied in this case. And for a while I did.

I passed my finals, worked at the lab and hung out with my roommates. The perfect summer until I got an urgent phone call from home weeks later.

"Ryn, I know you and Linna broke up after high school, but did you ever keep in touch with her?"

My mother had a way of getting right to the point. I had learned to be evasive.

"Why? What's going on?"

"Well, probably nothing you can help with. I mean, you're in Boston and she was in the D.C. area …"

"Yeah, so …"

"Her parents are calling all of the friends she had in school. Linna's gone missing. No one has seen her since she left Portland three weeks ago. Her cell phone was still in her Georgetown apartment, and it's as if she just disappeared. No signs of a struggle. Nothing. The police are treating it like a runaway at this point, but it doesn't make any sense to her parents."

I paused for a minute to let the news sink in.

"Ryn, are you still there?"

"Yeah, I'm here. I don't know what to tell you, Mom."

"Well, I didn't think you'd know anything. Still, I told the Sullivans I'd call. Such a shame. Anyhow,

Aeden's working as the play director for the YMCA Summer Camp and she seems to be enjoying it."

"Tell her I said hi. Same for Dad. And if I hear from Linna, I'll let you know. Bye, Mom."

I don't know how long I stood in the kitchen with the phone in my hand. But the next thing I knew, I was Googling "Lothian, Scotland, 1296."

Chapter Six:
Linna

*T*he tips of my fingers were ice cold and my feet were numb even though they were covered with thick woolen socks. It took me a minute or two to realize that I was lying face down in a light covering of snow. I could feel the wet grass underneath it. Ryn had said that I would be dizzy and disoriented. But I was neither. Just wet and cold. The last thing I remembered was an annoying buzzing sound followed by strobe lights. I kept hearing his voice over and over again, saying, "It's always cold in Scotland. It's always cold in Scotland."

You've got that right, Ryn. It is cold. I stood up and brushed the feathery white flakes from my clothing—a heavy brown knit dress that came down to my ankles and a thick black shawl that was long enough to wrap around my head twice. With the exception of my Doc Martens boots, that I bought online a few weeks ago, I was used to this outfit. I had worn it to dozens of Renaissance Festivals since junior high. But this was the real deal. No giant turkey legs or large pretzels. If I was lucky, someone might offer me bread and maybe a sip of mead. And that's the other thing. I wasn't nauseous. Maybe the vibrations in tandem with the light alleviated those side effects.

The air was heavy and damp with a steady wind, and the light flakes of snow circled my face like tiny stingers. *This has to be March or April. It couldn't be May. That would be too late.* I looked at the ground to see if anything was growing, but no signs of greenery poked their way through the snow. I smiled. It was the end of winter. I had arrived in time. And I arrived in the right place. But I arrived alone. I had wanted Ryn to travel back with me. It would have made things so much easier. I was being selfish and I knew it. He had wasted no time pointing that out.

"Are you kidding me? I don't want to be the third wheel on your date from beyond the grave. That's so… cold. No, you're on your own."

I pulled the shawl tighter across my chest and looked around. With its high tower and long, narrow windows, the abbey loomed over me as if it were some sort of mythical beast and I was its prey. *Well, what were you expecting? Cinderella's castle?* It was perched well above me on a small knoll, and I knew it would take at least a half hour or so to walk there. Not a risk worth taking considering the sun had just started to set in the murky, grey sky.

Off to my left was a small, thatched-roof cottage, nearly obscured by brush and piles of dirt. "They must be used to travelers seeking lodging on their way to the abbey," I thought as I started for the house. As I got closer I could see two children, maybe six or seven years old, playing by the front door. They were laughing and chasing each other. I waved as they looked my way. But they ignored me and continued with their game.

"Hoy! Gōdne æfen!" I yelled, hoping that I had gotten the greeting right for "good evening." And then something dawned on me. While I had translated Middle English and some Gaelic in literature, I had never actually heard it spoken. Apparently, I had gotten it wrong. The children screamed as if I were threatening their very lives and ran into the cottage. The heavy wooden door was slammed immediately.

Think fast, Linna. It's getting late and it's cold. I knew I'd have to pretend to be a traveler. Maybe with luck, the family inside would think that I came from some exotic place where their language wasn't spoken. It wasn't as if I had a choice. I had to get inside. Frostbite wasn't an option.

I pounded on the door and tried again. This time without the "hoy."

"Gōdne æfen."

The reply was loud and door remained shut.

"Stynthe!"

Stynthe. It meant "stop" or "cease." Why were they so afraid of me? I tried again. This time with a word that meant comfort or aid.

"Solas!"

Again the same reply, only louder.

"STYNTHE!"

And then, the most frightening of all replies.

"STYNTHE, GHAIST!"

Ghaist. Ghaist means ghost. Then, I realized something. They couldn't see me. That's why the children had screamed and ran. All they saw were my footprints in the snow. Something had gone wrong. Maybe by adding the vibrations to the formula I was obscured from their vision. Like one of those ceiling fans on full speed. Slowly, the blades can be seen, but when the fan is on high, it's as if the blades don't exist. I took a deep breath and bit my lower lip.

Stay calm. All of this will pass, eventually. But what about now? I was numb and thirsty. Scared and in need of shelter. Then it occurred to me. If they couldn't see me, maybe I was without form and could simply pass through the door like Dickens' ghost of Christmas past. I started to race towards the wooden frame shoulder first, but stopped within seconds. I did have form. I did have substance. Otherwise, I would not have been able to pound on the door. And, my voice could be heard. No wonder they thought I was an apparition.

I'd have to find another way into this cottage. And I needed to do it soon.

Chapter Seven:
The Abbey, 1296

The young monk had just completed the Matins prayers and returned to his bed. The narrow glass windows in the dormitory rattled from the wind, but none of the other monks seemed to notice. Sleep came easy for them, but not so for Brother Gregory. He pulled the thin woven blanket to his neck and closed his eyes. The chattering had gotten louder. Too late in the season for a winter storm, he thought, but it wasn't the wind that seemed to unnerve him. It was something else. Something sinister. A feeling perhaps? A premonition?

The monk slipped quietly from his bed and looked out the window. The snow was swirling with such intensity that all he could see were cloudy flakes illuminated by dim moonlight. He was about to turn away when a dark figure seemed to appear in the distance. He watched as it moved past the knoll to one of the cottages that surrounded the abbey.

Nothing to fear. Just someone looking for a lost sheep perhaps or in need of firewood. Then he caught sight of something else. Two Brothers walking through the courtyard that led from the dormitory to the wine cellar just below the refectory. The flickering of a small candle inside a lantern was the only light. Its beam bounced in the darkness with each step that the monk who was holding it took.

"A strange hour to go to the wine cellar," he said to himself. And then, that same feeling of foreboding came over him like a slow nausea. He swallowed the saliva in his mouth and stood still by the window, waiting for it to pass. The candlelight, along with the two monks, disappeared in the darkness.

Brother Gregory crossed himself and returned to his bed. In a few hours it would be daybreak and Prime Prayers would begin. But sleep never came. He felt a tightening in his chest and a strange choking feeling in his throat, as if a hand were pressing harder and harder around his neck. And every time his body started to drift off, the grip on his neck intensified.

Wrapping the blanket over his shoulders, the young monk knelt by his bed and prayed. At dawn he returned the blanket to the bed and walked slowly to the latrine before making his way to the nave of the church. The silence, which had always been a comfort to him, seemed to harbor a voice of its own. A voice that was more warning than the mustering of any words.

Chapter Eight: Linna

The wooden slats on the windows were bolted from inside and there was no way I was going to get into that cottage. But another one stood a good 150 or so yards in the distance, on the edge of a narrow berm. I could make it to that one if I moved quickly.

My legs were starting to feel stiff and the intensifying wind didn't make things any easier. I took large strides and pushed myself forward until I was standing in front of another heavy wooden door. This time I didn't knock. I pulled the round brass knob towards me, hoping that whoever was inside had not bothered to bolt it. I was quick. Quicker than I ever thought I could be. In an instant I was standing in a small dark room whose only occupants were an old man and a young girl. A small fireplace and two cots were the only discernible furnishings. The girl rushed to the door and bolted it just as I moved against the wall. She said something to the elderly man, whom I assumed was her father.

"Pyff byre."

I repeated the phrase to myself until I realized what she meant. "A puff of strong wind." Well, at least she wasn't screaming about ghosts or banshees, but I knew I had to stay out of their way, and it wasn't going to be easy in such a small space. I angled myself closer to the fire. By now I was unbearably cold and needed any kind of warmth. I figured that once they went to their cots for the night I could sleep near the fireplace on the floor. I had to be close enough to one of the walls so that they wouldn't trip over me.

As my eyes got accustomed to the faint light in the room emanating from the hearth, I could see a small table with a loaf of bread on it and a few pieces of fruit. Dinner, if they fell asleep fast enough. Surely, a torn off piece of bread wouldn't be missed. They'd think the other one ate it. But could I stand that long?

My feet were tired and even leaning against the wall was no help. I spotted a small stool and crept towards it. I sat gingerly, trying not to make a sound. I'd have to remain in this position until the man and his daughter went to sleep.

The fact that I wasn't visible to anyone was really creepy. I tried not to dwell on it. It occurred to me that I could use it to my advantage. In spite of the fact that I had plotted out a means to get here, I hadn't really formulated a plan for entering the abbey. Initially, I thought I could pose as a traveler, but there weren't many, if any, women traveling alone. Then I figured I could swipe a monk's garb from the monastery and pretend to be a boy. Not that farfetched.

I was on the thin side and even though I was certainly developed, I had to admit that my curves were on the subtle side. With my hair cut short, no makeup and a monk's robe, I could pass for a boy or young man. But now, none of that mattered. I had a way in. No one would see me. I just had to wait till morning and then make my way up to the abbey. In the meantime, I sat as still as I could and tried to piece together what they were saying.

The names were clear—King John Balliol and Edward I. If I got my history facts straight, Edward I was the King of England, and he had appointed John Balliol as the reigning king of Scotland. That was all I remembered. But from what I was hearing, something had gone wrong with that arrangement.

It was like listening to a song in another language where you knew some of the words but not all of them.

"Folcgewinn … gefeoht ... herebróga …"

Something about war and battle. But "herebróga" stood out. I must have come across that word in an old poem years ago. I just couldn't seem to place it. I tried to focus on what the man and his daughter were saying.

John Balliol had reneged on his allegiance to King Edward and was siding with the French. The man seemed scared, and given the reaction from his daughter, she was even more frightened. I clenched my hands and listened.

Then I heard that word again. Herebróga. Only this time it clicked. The word didn't just mean war or battle. It was the *dread* of war. Something was about to happen, and I was going to be right in the middle of it.

The fire was starting to go out and the room began to get cold. The man and his daughter moved to their cots and I closed my eyes. I could see the loaf of bread a few feet from me. I'd make my move when I was sure they were asleep.

There was more to fear in the little cottage than ghosts.

Chapter Nine:
The Abbey, 1296

The two monks walked silently in single file down the spiraling staircase that led from the wine cellar to a labyrinth of alcoves and small rooms. They were familiar with this secret part of the abbey. Still, they relied on the faint light from a solitary candle inside a small lantern to illuminate the way. Bending their heads so as not to hit the low ceiling, they moved through a winding tunnel until they reached a small room that housed only a wooden table and bench.

Lifting the seat from the bench, one of the monks took out a few pieces of wood that had been sanded and a carving tool. He handed the other monk a small glass jar sealed with wax and a thin brush.

"It will be a long night," he said as he placed the lantern on the table.

"We have broken our vows. We must pray for salvation," was the response.

"We do this so that others may keep their vows."

"And if we are found out?"

"We've spoken of this before. Then we sacrifice one life in order to save generations. God grant it never comes to that."

The monks remained silent as they began their task—one carving the detailed drawing of St. John the Baptist on the smooth piece of wood while the other added color and depth to another piece.

"We should have this completed by the next full moon," the first monk said. "And then it's just a matter of adding the contents."

"Does the girl know where to find us?"

"She knows the appointed time to be at the cloister wall. Her father will send word to King John's men."

"It seems a barter more of the devil than the Lord."

"Deceit, yes. But of the devil, no. It is the only way to assure the monastery survives."

When the candle had melted to within a quarter of its length, the monks cleared the table, placing their work back in the bench. The echo of their footsteps faded as they reached the wine cellar.

With a quick breath, the candlelight was extinguished and the monks made their way back to the dormitory. And while their feet glided noiselessly on the wooden floor, their breathing was short and labored. In the stillness of the room someone had heard them. Someone who held the thin woolen blanket to his neck and trembled beneath it.

Chapter Ten:
Linna

I left the cottage before anyone woke up, but not before tearing off a small piece of bread and taking one of the reddish-yellow apples that were on the table. It was the first time in my life that I had stolen anything. Well, not exactly the first. When I was five years old my father had taken me to a circus performance and a vendor had brought a tray of hotdogs to the people sitting in front of us. I reached my hand out between the seats, grabbed a hotdog and stuffed it in my mouth before my father could say anything. I imagine he paid the vendor for the price of my meal and apologized to the people, but I honestly don't remember that part.

There was no way I could pay these people or apologize for that matter without scaring the daylights out of them. Ryn hadn't warned me about the decisions I'd have to make in circumstances that I couldn't control. But in fairness, he did warn me about everything else.

It was still bitter cold outside, but the sun was up and a light coating of snow had crystalized on the ground, concealing any traces of green on the knoll that led to the abbey. In the distance I could see a wooded area and some rock formations, but mostly the land was rolling fields and small hills. I began to climb the berm at a steady pace, hoping that if there was someone around they wouldn't notice the phantom footsteps in the snow. I had to admit, that would have freaked me out, too.

As I got closer to the monastery I could see a small water mill and thatched barns. It appeared as if milk cows and sheep were roaming freely while a few goats were penned up near one of the barns. No one was in sight and I kept walking until I reached a stone walkway surrounding a square garden. Just past the walkway was a bell tower and the church itself, large and cross-shaped. The hum of voices seemed to get louder, and I realized that the monks were probably deep in prayer for the first mass of the day.

Good, Linna. This gives you time to scope out the rest of the abbey. Start moving. The courtyard led to smaller hallways and rooms. Some unadorned with wooden tables and chairs while others had silver chalices and candlesticks on top of carefully draped white linens. I kept moving. *So this is what Harry Potter must have felt like with that invisibility cloak. At least I don't have to worry about letting something like that slip off of me.* I found the dormitory next. It was upstairs, directly above a large empty room with arches and columns. I knew it was the dormitory—lots of narrow cots all lined up in one large room with long windows. From there I found some sort of sitting room and what looked like a specialized area for writing. *Was this where I could find my monk?*

Other than the soft hum of voices from across the courtyard, everything around me was silent. I went back downstairs, walked outside and made my way to the kitchen. Again, devoid of people. But there were plenty of pots with potatoes and vegetables as well as a large oven that was still warm. *At least I won't starve here.*

In an instant, I heard a scuffling sound. Turning around quickly I could see that a few of the monks had returned to the kitchen. *Quick, Linna! Get out of their way!* I all but fell on top of one of the tables as I made a move towards the oven. If I had hoped to get information by eavesdropping on them, I was wrong. No one spoke. They just went about their business as if the place was a beehive and all the insects knew what they were doing. Then, I noticed something. Subtle at first. They had a means of sign language.

Splendid! As if trying to figure out Middle English wasn't enough, now I'd need a course in medieval signing!

It was amusing in a bizarre sort of way. I tried to imagine what they were saying when suddenly I saw something that didn't need any translation. A tall, heavy-set monk walked directly in front of another monk who had just placed some peeled potatoes into a pot. And unless he was complaining about the food, the message he delivered sent a cold chill through my body.

He lifted his head and glanced upward before taking his thumb and running it across his neck. The universal language for murder.

Chapter Eleven:
The Abbey, 1296

Brother Gregory could barely remain awake at supper and much to his chagrin found himself dozing during the evening Compline service. His body seemed to sink into the small cot and within minutes he was fast asleep. His eyes still burned from hours of work in the Scriptorium. The curve of each letter had to be exact. Perfect. This was not a task where one could make mistakes.

His breathing was slow and steady. Unlike the night before, sleep came immediately. The young monk had only moved once during the night before returning to his usual position. He liked the idea of facing the ceiling of the room with Heaven above him. But then, everything changed.

Was it a sound or an aroma that he couldn't place? But whatever woke him, it sent a chill down his neck, and he could feel tiny goose bumps on his flesh. Brother Gregory glanced around the dormitory. It was silent and still. Yet something wasn't right. He stood up carefully, placing one foot at a time on the floor, and walked slowly to the cot where Brother Jarvin had slept. For some inexplicable reason, the young monk was certain that the cot was occupied even though he knew that Brother Jarvin had died less than two weeks ago.

He could see that the bed was empty. The muted moonlight cast a grey beam across the room, illuminating the cots closest to his own. Still, Brother Gregory could feel his hands shaking as he returned to his own place in the room. He sat at the edge of his bed and stared across the room as if he were waiting for something to appear. And that's when the flickering light bounced across the narrow windows.

Brother Gregory tiptoed to the edge of the nearest window and peered through the glass. The same figures of two monks crossed the courtyard and headed into the wine cellar. He started to turn around when he felt a soft, warm breath at the back of his neck. Instinctively, he moved his arm but there was nothing there. And then, he heard it. Clear and unmistakable. The sound of footsteps on the wide wooden planks in his dormitory, but no one was walking.

Crossing himself and saying a quick prayer, the young monk followed the noise of the footsteps to the steep narrow staircase that took him from the dormitory to the open room below. He hadn't stopped to take the candle from his bedside. He knew every inch of the stairwell and no light was needed.

The footsteps seemed softer as they moved from the inner parlor to the open courtyard. Still, Brother

Gregory had no trouble staying within a few feet of the noise. Suddenly, the sound stopped. They were in the outer courtyard where soft grass covered with light snow replaced the old wooden planks of the monastery floor. The area was empty and silent. Only the footprints of the two monks who had walked across to the wine cellar remained visible in the moonlight.

Blinking his eyes, Brother Gregory stared directly across the snow-covered square. He became acutely aware of something. New footprints were emerging on the grass. A specter? An illusion? He dropped to his knees and began to pray until he finally had the courage to cross the courtyard and go into the barrel-making area that led to the wine cellar.

The large room was empty except for a few wooden barrels. Sufficient moonlight from three rounded windows allowed the young monk to study his surroundings. Nothing unusual except for tiny droplets of candlewax on the floor. Brother Gregory took a quick breath and moved forward until he reached a tight, winding staircase. Placing each hand on the side walls, he took one slow step at a time until he could go no further. He had reached the base of the stairs. With no light to guide him, he waited until his eyes got accustomed to the darkness.

Taking a tentative step, Brother Gregory started to move through the winding labyrinth. He was certain that he could hear muffled voices, but where? Each hallway led to another and another. Or worse yet, to a dead end.

All of a sudden the temperature around him seemed to change, as if something was warming the air. But all he could discern were passageways and alcoves, until at last he saw a flickering lantern light. It stopped him dead in his tracks and meant only one thing—he was in danger. If he could see the wavering light, then whoever had carried it to this place could see him as well.

Chapter Twelve:
Linna

I had become the phantom thief, stealing bits and pieces of food from the kitchen before ultimately winding up in the room that had to be the Scriptorium. Its alcoves were filled with books and decorated scrolls. And on the small wooden tables were jars of inks and assorted quill pens. Pieces of parchment and portions of scrolls were carefully placed so as not to be disturbed by anyone except the scribe who was copying the text.

The room was empty. The monks were still at prayer. I had no idea that it took up so much of their day. *Honestly, Linna. What did you think?* But formal prayers meant one thing for me. I could use that time to poke around at each table and study the text. I knew the one that I was translating in Georgetown. If I could find it, I could figure out which monk was the one who was about to be killed. Of course, there was something else. Something I didn't want to admit.

Damn it, Ryn. Maybe you were right. Maybe I have the teeniest, tiniest bit of a crush on this guy. Okay, so I've said it. So what?

Much as I didn't want to say it, I honestly thought that if I saw this monk, I would recognize him immediately. Like one of those romance novels where the heroine knows in a split second that she is standing face to face with her one true love.

Pull yourself together, Linna. You sound like you're in ninth grade, not a college intern!

But would I know him? Could I recognize him? Only if I believed in fairytales. I walked over to the first table and studied the parchment—a detailed prayer for Vespers. Not my monk. The second table wasn't my monk either. Someone was drawing what appeared to be a large flowery capital letter P in reds, greens and yellows. Again, not my monk. I managed to study three other tables before I heard a noise and had to retreat to the corner of the room. The scribes were returning.

One by one they filed into the room and took their places at the tables. The soft scuttling sound of their feet on the wood floor was the only hint of life. The room remained still even as they worked. I was standing on a side wall when they entered, so I couldn't really see their faces. And I was afraid that if I did make a move I'd knock into something. Those tables were spaced so close to each other that there was hardly room to stretch.

From my vantage point I could see that the top of their heads was shaved. Perfect round circles. The thought of Friar Tuck entered my mind and I stifled a giggle. Finally, I got the courage to move against the wall until I reached the front of the room where I could see their faces. Most of their heads were bent down, inches from the parchment. Unless I got really close up and personal, it was impossible to get a good look. I tried moving to the other wall, but that was no help either. *And you thought this was going to be so easy. Ryn's probably laughing by now.*

And then I had a better idea. I would wait in the narrow hallway when they exited the room. That way I would be able to see their faces. Unfortunately, I was wrong. By the time they left the Scriptorium what little natural light there was in the hallway had faded. *I hope I'm never asked to point someone out in a police lineup.*

Once the monks left the hallway they dispersed in all different directions. Some to the courtyard, others to the church and still others to a large meeting room adjacent to the cloisters. I decided to follow the ones who went into the meeting room, but after a few minutes I came to the conclusion that my monk was not among them.

That left the courtyard, but only three elderly monks were seated on the benches around the square. The church was straight ahead, so I wasted no time entering it. *Another stupid move, Linna. The monks are all kneeling and unless you think you can climb over a few pews, you won't see their faces.*

It was ridiculous. Futile. I didn't have a plan or even a coherent thought. I was tired, hungry and uncomfortable. I had forgotten how itchy and cumbersome my outfit was. But it wasn't as if I had other options. *It's always cold in Scotland.* I needed that heavy garb even if I was invisible to everyone around me. I pulled the shawl closer to me and caught a whiff of mildew. How long had this thing been in my closet? And, could anyone else smell it?

I returned to the courtyard and watched as a few monks puttered around what appeared to be a small herb garden in the far corner. They brushed bits of crusty snow from the buds, each man alone in his own thoughts. No conversation. No laughter. Nothing. Just slow and seamless movements. I should have found it peaceful. Serene. But it was as if I was watching a charade. I couldn't quite explain it, but something was off.

Without warning, a bell sounded and the monks gathered from all corners of the abbey and moved slowly into the church. Another service. Another chance to study their faces. But that too, proved futile.

By the end of the day I was exhausted, itchy and hungry. I managed to find a bit of hard cheese and some greens. If nothing else, maybe when I get back I can write a new diet book—*The Monastery Diet.* It might even make the best-sellers list. *Don't get your hopes up, Linna. Someone probably wrote one. And didn't monks write about training dogs as well?*

When the monks finally went to their dormitory, I followed and waited until I was sure that they had gone to sleep. In the candlelight I could see that all of the beds had thin pillows and a blanket. All but one. It was empty. Probably an extra in case someone decided to join the order. *Well, Goldilocks, what are you waiting for?* I sat down slowly and leaned back, lifting my legs until I was lying flat on my back.

I knew that monks had taken vows of poverty and chastity. But misery? Sleeping in that cot meant an entirely different oath. Still, it was a bed, and I needed some rest. Closing my eyes, I began to feel comfortable in the darkness. Rhythmic breathing coupled with the creaking of the beds assured me that there was life in this room. I let myself drift off. And then, without warning, I felt my body tighten and my eyes flew open. Someone was approaching the bed.

Breathe slowly, Linna. Breathe softly. You know that feeling you get when you're just coming out of a dream and your body can't move? That's exactly how I felt, only I wasn't dreaming. Someone was staring at me. I moved my head slowly, but by the time I could look, I saw someone returning to his bed. Then, the flickering started. Lights outside in the courtyard. I got up and moved to the window.

Two figures were holding a candle and walking across the yard. I had serious doubts that they were going to pray, and even though it went against everything I've been taught, I stood up from the bed and started slowly across the room until I reached the stairs. Then, I raced down as fast as I could so that by the time I reached the outside, I could still see them.

Past the small herb garden, past the cloister wall, the two men kept moving, and I was close behind. We entered a large rectangular room with wooden barrels and slats of rounded wood. Their candle gave off enough light for me to keep pace. Next, they headed down a steep circular stairwell into the wine cellar and from there, yet another, narrower staircase.

Good going, Linna. Following two strangers to God-knows-where. Maybe next time you'd like to get into a car with an axe murderer. I swore I could hear my mother's voice.

I had the strangest sensation that I was being followed. If it wasn't bad enough being inches from something sinister, I was beginning to feel as if a trap was closing in on me. *Just keep breathing, Linna.*

The light kept bouncing as we walked through twisting tunnels and tight alcoves until we had reached a doorway to a small room. I could see a single table and one of the monks placing the candle down before turning his head towards the door. At that instant, he gasped.

Had they seen me? Did the vibrations slow down long enough for me to become visible? I cringed as I took a quick breath. I heard them speak, and I realized they weren't talking about me. A few feet behind me stood a young monk. And I knew then that he wasn't supposed to see what the others were doing in this room.

In a blink everything became clear to me. The monk had followed me. He had sensed my presence. *Stupid, Linna. Stupid. Your footprints in the snow led him to this place.* Sure, I could rationalize that his curiosity upon seeing the flickering candlelight was what brought him to this secret room under the wine cellar. But I knew otherwise. It was me. My footsteps in the snow. And if the man standing behind me was *my* monk, then I may have unwittingly caused the one thing I went back in time to prevent.

Chapter Thirteen:
Ryn

I had just pulled up a map of Scotland on my smartphone when I felt it vibrate. Damn it! A text from Aeden. It was as if my sister could read my mind.

"3 wks is a long time to B gone. What do U really know?"

I texted back.

"Nothing."

She replied.

"Liar."

Then I turned off the phone and walked over to the fridge for a Coke. Aeden was going to be persistent and I knew it. She'd text. She'd phone, and worse yet, she'd text and phone my roommates until I reached a breaking point. The only good thing about any of this was that she was still in Portland and her fall term wouldn't begin for another four weeks. I grabbed a half-eaten ham and cheese sandwich that I was sure was mine before heading back to the lab.

Only one other tech was in the lab when I walked in.

"Hey Ryn, someone left a message for you. She was talking so fast I only jotted down what I thought was important. I figured it was an old girlfriend and you didn't want to give her your number."

Linna! Was she back? Was everything okay?

"Where's the message? What did she say?"

"Whoa! You're almost as manic as she was! It's on the counter by that stack of papers you've been working on."

I grabbed the torn off piece of paper and started to read it. Crap! It was Aeden. And it was really bad news.

"Flying in next week. Camp over. Costume inventory. We need to talk."

"Did my sister mention when she was flying in?" I yelled across the room.

"That was your sister? And the answer is no, she didn't give a date. But she sure was in overdrive. I never heard anyone talk that fast. She should learn how to text."

"Uh huh," I muttered, ignoring the last comment. I was too preoccupied thinking about the last four words. *"We need to talk."*

It's always bad when someone says that, no matter who it is.

"We need to talk, Ryn. This letter says you've had 12 detentions."

"We need to talk, Ryn. Camp is out of the question this summer. We need to clean out Auntie Zanne's house in Arizona."

"We need to talk, Ryn. Sorry about the lacrosse meet. Your great uncle died and we need to straighten out a few of his things."

And my list could go on. But when the someone who says, "We need to talk" is my sister, I know it's the opening line for a disaster.

And so there I was, eight days later in another coffee shop, this one close to her college. I had hoped that maybe the bridges over the Charles River would be closed down, but no such luck. The Orange Line was still running, and my bus was on time. Aeden rushed to greet me as soon as I stepped into The Thinking Cup. Leave it to her to find a place that sounded academic.

"Wow! You found the place right away! Come on, let's get a seat."

I ordered two coffees and sat down at a corner table. It wasn't a particularly busy time of the day, but I still didn't want to be in earshot of anyone.

"Okay, Aeden. You dragged me all the way over from Cambridge so this better be good. What's going on?"

"Maybe you should tell me. Linna's been gone for what? Weeks now? Don't tell me you don't know anything about it because Mom already spoke to you."

"Look Aeden, so yeah, I did see Linna last month but only for a few minutes, and I really don't know where she is at this very minute."

Technically, it wasn't a lie.

"You know something," Aeden said. "I can tell. And as long as I'm at it, I might as well tell you something. I think Linna knew about the prisms and Snell's Law. Enough to get her in trouble."

"Go on."

"It was a long time ago. You were probably a Junior. Both of you were studying for some test and I saw you walking into the kitchen. Linna was alone in your room and when I went past the door, she was reading all your notes on time travel. The ones you kept on your desk under that ridiculous paperweight of the flying pig. I never bothered to say anything because that would have made me a sneak. Besides, I was sure she'd say something to you."

"Listen Aeden, I—"

"She's gone missing for a long time. No sign of a struggle. Linna just vanished. I'll tell you what I think. Your ex-girlfriend stumbled across something and used your notes to go back in time. Well? Am I right or not? And don't lie to me."

"Wouldn't dream of it, Aeden. Drink your coffee and keep your voice low."

Chapter Fourteen:
Linna

*T*his was all my fault and I had to do something. The dim candlelight was enough to illuminate the features of the two monks who were near the table. Both had thin, gaunt faces, but one had deep-set wrinkles and a dark mole by the corner of his nose. The light was strong enough for me to see some sort of box that they were studying. The men seemed to be pre-occupied with it, but it was only a matter of time until they noticed the visitor by the stairwell. And it would be total chaos if *that* monk, *my* monk, started to move forward. He'd bump into me and who knows what would happen. So, against everything that was ever drilled into my head by my parents, I acted on the first thing that came to my mind.

I ran over to the candle and blew it out. Puff! In an instant—total darkness. Total darkness in a labyrinth under a wine cellar.

What's the matter with you, Linna! You need to think things through. You can't just act impulsively. Man was meant to reason, not react.

Now, in the pitch black I had to find my way out. Behind me the footsteps of the young monk got faster and faster. He was making his way out of here. At least the others hadn't seen his face. But what if they caught up? Darkness or not, these men knew their way around the cellars, while I was totally lost and disoriented.

Use your senses, Linna. That's why you've got them in the first place.

I took a deep breath and focused on the sounds. Everyone had moved from the small room. I placed my arms out in front of me and swept them around so I wouldn't bump into anything as I forced my feet to keep moving. Narrow corridors, musty odors, and enough twists and turns to rival any funhouse. I swore I'd never go back to this place.

Then I heard noises that meant only one thing. Stairs! The footsteps were going up and I followed. At the landing to the wine cellar, I could make out shadows and movement. Even though we were still underground, the moonlight from the windows above us crept through the ceiling beams and offered just enough light to turn the blackness into a thin grey haze.

I watched as the shadowy figures walked out into the courtyard, but I couldn't tell if there were two or three of them, and by the time I moved past the cloister wall and into the monastery itself, it was too late. Everyone had disappeared. And oddly enough, there were no sounds of footsteps or any other indication that anyone was out and about.

I stopped and caught my breath.

This is just the beginning, Linna. They'll come looking for him, and blowing out a candle isn't going to save him.

I didn't want to return to the dormitory. Somehow, it just didn't feel right. Maybe it was a gut instinct, but whatever it was, something told me to go back to the room under the cellar. I had to find out what those monks had inside that box. I would need to know if I was ever going to help my monk. And then I realized something. What if the monk who was behind me in that stairwell wasn't my monk after all? What made me think it was him in the first place? All of this was getting way too confusing.

Was this how Alice in Wonderland felt when she stumbled all around? Heck, Linna. At least she had a plan. She was following a rabbit. Who are you following?

I wanted to cry. Seriously break down and sob. But I was too tired and too cold. Maybe I'd come up with something if I could just get some sleep.

The small parlor room faced the courtyard and I went inside. Propping myself against two corner walls, I pulled my shawl over my mouth and breathed my own warm breath. It was the only comfort I had as I closed my eyes and waited for morning.

Chapter Fifteen:
Ryn

If anyone could make a production out of drinking a cup of coffee, it was Aeden. First one sugar, then two, then more cream, then another taste. I just watched her as I tried to figure out what to say next. When I was sure she had some liquid in her mouth, I spoke.

"Here's the deal. And don't jump in until I'm finished. I really don't know where Linna is exactly, but I have an idea. She was translating a 13th-century Latin liturgy as part of her internship."

Aeden gave me a blank look as if to say, "So?"

"Anyway, she found some encrypted messages in the text, and they were about a monk getting murdered or about to get murdered."

Aeden's jaw dropped open and she put the coffee cup down without even looking at the table.

"You don't think …"

"Yeah, I do. In fact, I'm sure of it. Linna's kind of gone off the deep end over that monk. It's like she's obsessed with him or something."

"What did she say?"

"The usual junk. About how sensitive he was, how poetic, how… Oh, I don't know. The guy sounded like a brooding melancholy poet if you ask me, but apparently that's what turns Linna on lately. And don't give me that look, Aeden. I'm totally over her."

"She's going to try to stop him from getting murdered, isn't she? She's figured it out. Snell's Law. The refraction. The whole time travel thing."

I just nodded and let my sister continue.

"Oh my God, Ryn. That's so romantic!"

Then it was as if someone had slapped her in the face because all of sudden her expression changed.

"A monk. A 13th-century monk. From where? England? France? Germany? Oh please, tell me it's Spain. I always wanted to go to Spain. So how do you think Linna got the money to fly over there?"

"First of all, it wasn't Spain, it was Scotland. And Linna didn't fly over there."

"I don't get it. Did she go back in time or not?"

"Ever hear the expression, '*everyone knows something someone else doesn't know?*' Well, in this case, Linna knew about dimensionality in space."

"Like moving horizontally as well as linearly in time?"

"Yep, she found a new component to our formulas. This one for vibrations that could move you to another place in time."

I saw it coming. Aeden was about to shriek. And given her recent flair for the dramatic, I knew she was going to make a scene. I had to do something. Anything. I jumped up and knocked her coffee cup off the table and onto her lap, spilling the lukewarm cream and sugar mixture all over her. At least if she was going to scream, it would be for a reason people would understand.

"What the hell, Ryn!"

"I'm sorry. Here. Take a napkin."

Aeden snatched a handful of them from the small condiment bench near us and sat down. I whispered as she tried to sop up the sticky liquid.

"I think Linna's in Scotland. 1296 to be exact. At a monastery in Lothian, near Edinburgh."

"But she should have been back by now. Time never lapses that long."

"Maybe the vibrations altered the time-space continuum."

"You think she's stuck?"

I shrugged and answered her.

"Either that or the guy quit the order, and they lived happily ever after."

"Cut it out. You know that she'll get forced back to her own time. Even if that monk turns out to be her one true love."

"For Heaven's sake, Aeden. You've been hanging out in the theater department too long!"

"So, do you intend to do something or not? Mom said that Linna's parents were flying to D.C. to close up her apartment. It's too bad we can't get our hands on her computer or anything she wrote for that matter. Well, yes or no?"

"No. Not yet, anyway. Linna wouldn't want me there, and besides, I'm not so sure I'd want to be. And don't you get any ideas about going back in time to watch theater performances all over the world! Rent a DVD or something."

"If Linna's not back by Halloween, I say we try the new formula."

"I'll think about it when you learn how to say '*Trick or Treat*' in Latin. And sorry about your clothes, Aeden. Hope you don't have to be anywhere special."

"Not yet!"

Chapter Sixteen:
Linna

A sudden twitch and I awoke with a start. The darkness outside was starting to give way to morning. If I hurried, I could get to the cellar before anyone else was out and about. My body felt tight and rigid as I stood up, and for some reason my legs moved slower than usual. I started for the courtyard when I noticed something out of place. Something that wasn't there yesterday. I was staring at a large shape on the ground near the corner with the herb garden. A deer perhaps? Or maybe someone's dog that wandered in?

I walked slowly, cautiously, trying to keep my distance. No need to get a dog barking, or worse. I had to pass that area in order to get to the wine cellar. And even if I wasn't visible, I would still be noticed if it was a dog. My scent would give me away. I took slow, deliberate steps. Only a few more feet and the path would veer off. Yet something wasn't right. My footsteps would have scared a deer and they most certainly would have alerted even the laziest of canines. I turned and looked back at the ground.

And that's when I heard myself gasp. It was a body. The body of a monk. *Oh my God! I'm too late. They've killed him. Pull yourself together, Linna. It might not be him. Go over there. Take a look. Move your feet, Linna.*

My hands were shaking and my feet felt frozen in place. I don't even remember how long it took me to walk over to the body, but when I did, I recognized the man immediately. It was the monk with the long, thin face and mole near his nose. Only now, a thin line of blood had frozen in place underneath his nostril. And two smaller lines of blood framed the bottom of his chin like a hideous marionette waiting for its puppet master to pull the strings. I moved my hand to my mouth and stood there. Other than the small amount of blood on the monk's face there was no sign of struggle. No visible wounds. No blood on his robe. No rope wrapped around his neck or any bruising for that matter. And even though I was no expert on heart failure, this didn't appear to be a heart attack. The monk's eyes were wide open. Vapid. Vacant. Glassy. I turned away.

Look around you, Linna. It's getting lighter outside. Hurry up and look. Look for any clues. Your monk might be next if this one was murdered.

I forced myself to take another look. I'd never seen a dead body before. And the few funerals that I had attended were all closed-casket. Bending down slightly to get a better look, I saw a small pool of blood coming from behind one of the man's ears.

Tilt his head, Linna. You're not going to get another chance. He's dead. He can't hurt you.

My hand shook as my palm rested on his chin and lifted his head slightly. There, on the back of his neck, was a small puncture wound as if someone stabbed him with a sharp dagger or cutting knife. The wound was black around the edges. Maybe the blood had just dried there. Still, it didn't look like the color of dried blood. But I'm no forensic expert. Blood is blood and dead is dead. By now my entire body was shaking and I could actually hear myself breathing.

Calm down, Linna. At least you know one thing. He was murdered.

The courtyard was absolutely still. In a matter of minutes the daily routine of the abbey would begin. A bell would ring and monks would file to the church, but not before finding this one, dead on the ground. I had to move fast if I had any chance of getting to the cellar and finding out what that box contained. I couldn't risk having anyone hear me, even if they couldn't see me.

By the time the first chime rang I was already down the stairwell from the wine cellar and into the winding hallways. At least now there was some muted light from the floorboards above. Still, I had to watch my step. More dead ends, tight alcoves and narrow passages until I finally reached the room. The box was still sitting on the table, and as I held it in my hands I couldn't fathom what on earth made it so valuable that these monks would sneak down here in the middle of the night.

Even in the scant light I could see that it was carved with images of knights bearing swords. At either end were crosses and a large crucifix. The lid wobbled a bit and the box fell open. Empty. Nothing inside. No valuables. Just an empty wooden box. Then why the secrecy? And did it have anything to do with that monk's death and possibly the murder of another monk?

I moved my hand to steady the bench that was in front of the table and inadvertently lifted the wooden seat. *Oh my gosh—a storage bench. A 13th-century storage bench!* Quickly, I lifted the lid all the way up and looked inside. Too dark to tell, but it wasn't empty.

Be careful Linna. You don't know what you're touching. I could feel something thin like a pencil, only smooth on the cylinder part but sharp and gritty at the ends. Moving it closer to the light from the ceiling floorboards I took a good look. A bone. A piece of bone. Animal bone? Or…what? There were other pieces of bone as well. Different shapes, but small, fragile bones.

For a minute I could almost hear Ryn's voice. *"Probably some monk's gambling game. No one can spend the entire day praying. They didn't have dice so they had to resort to bones."*

Ryn. He always had a way of making me laugh. Even now. I put the piece of bone back in the bench and expected it to rattle the wood, but it didn't. It was cushioned. Reaching my hand in further, I felt a swatch of soft, smooth hair. Hair! Bones resting on hair! And in that split second, I knew exactly what I was holding. Anyone who studied anything about the Crusades knew about this stuff. I cringed. To perpetrate a charade like this in a monastery was unthinkable. Worse yet, was it the reason my monk was about to be killed? I closed the lid and stepped away. The muted light was getting stronger. That meant it was daylight and by now someone had found the body in the courtyard.

I tried to reason things out, but it was all a garble in my mind. A clandestine, greedy act. One dead monk and one monk scared that he's next. This couldn't be a coincidence. I knew that no one was going to talk. Especially in an abbey where the monks have taken a vow of silence. But not everyone speaks with words. I just needed to know how to listen.

When I reached the top of the stairs into the wine cellar, I could hear the commotion coming from the courtyard. Within seconds I was standing near the cloister wall watching as four monks placed the dead body on a plank of wood and started to move the man into the church.

If my knowledge of the Middle Ages was right, then that box was about to be moved, too. What I didn't know, as I stared at the macabre procession, was that I would be the one to move the box and its questionable contents.

Chapter Seventeen:
Ryn

*T*he envelope arrived by priority mail. Postmarked October 3rd from Portland. I knew what it was the minute I saw the return address. Linna always had a way of covering her tracks, only this time she wasn't the one who sent it. The handwriting for the return address wasn't hers.

Inside, the letter was brief and to the point.

"Ryn, we are certain you know by now that Linna has not been seen or heard from in months. For some reason, she wanted these notes to be sent to you. They were stacked neatly on her desk in Georgetown with the words 'please give this information to Ryn.' Taped to the note was the enclosed flash drive. The police reviewed the contents, but it was just her translations of some Latin text—a project she was working on at school. Not sure what this means to you but we are abiding by her wishes.

Our best to your sister in Boston. Have a successful school term and thank you for being such a good friend to our daughter."

It was signed *Mrs. Londra Sullivan.*

The notes were photocopies of the actual parchment—ornate, embellished and impossible for me to figure out. I thought I'd have better luck with the flash drive, but I was wrong. I only had one year of Latin and that was a junior high disaster. *Why the hell couldn't you translate something in French, Linna? I speak and read French fluently! Damn it, Linna! Latin of all things!*

I stared at the jumble of letters on my computer screen and shook my head. Only a Latin scholar would have a clue. And M.I.T. was not exactly the breeding ground for anyone majoring in the classics. But Harvard was. And their Classics Department was just across the river. Another fun ride on the Orange Line. I immediately went to Google, made a few phone calls, and 50 minutes later I actually talked to someone. A doctoral candidate by the name of Charlotte Campbell, who was willing to meet with me.

Yeah, I still had it bad for Linna Sullivan. Bad enough to tie up a Friday afternoon with some Latin scholar at Harvard.

Chapter Eighteen:
Linna

I followed closely as the four monks moved the body into a small room just past the sanctuary. Wordless, they gathered basins of water, removed his clothes and washed him. A preparation for burial. So much for gathering evidence of his murder. It was as if they had ignored that fact completely.

As I turned to head back to the courtyard, I could see the shadow of another monk in the archway. So much for a quick exit. Looking around the small room, I noticed another archway, this one in the far corner. With no other options, I walked through it, finding myself in a narrow passageway illuminated by small vertical windows near the ceiling. *This parallels the courtyard. I just need to keep going.*

It happened in an instant. Just like fan blades coming to a complete halt. I bumped head-on into someone who had entered the passageway from the other side. And that's the moment the vibrations caught up with time, and I was no longer a ghost.

Two hands grasped my wrists and the man leaned forward and spoke. I strained to understand his words—

a combination of Middle English and Gaelic. He repeated them. And even though I wasn't sure of the exact translation, the sharpness and anger in his tone was apparent.

"You have come too soon. Later. After dark."

Then, before I could even catch my breath, he grabbed my arm and moved me quickly down the hall and out a small alcove that faced the field behind the abbey.

"Go! Go! Later. After dark."

I was being sent away. Banished by a haggard looking monk with deep-set furrows in his forehead. As we stood in the doorway, I realized that he was the other monk who had been hiding that box. It was his friend who had been murdered. But he didn't appear to be mourning. Or even in shock, for that matter. He shoved me out the door with a push of the arm and spoke again.

"Go! Go! Later. After dark."

Exhausted from little to no sleep, hungry from lack of food, and petrified that my monk would be the next body found face up in the courtyard, I stood there dazed for a moment. The man in the dark robe gave me a quick shove this time, turned and walked back into the hall.

I thought monks were kind and gentle people. So much for that.

There was no way I could return to the monastery. Not in plain sight anyway. But the man did say "later."

He said "æfterweard" and that meant a later time. It was as if he was expecting me, only after dark. *After dark* could be anytime in the night. Meanwhile, I needed a place to stay, some food and maybe even water to wash my face. The only places I knew of were those small thatched cottages that dotted the hills behind this place. I just had to keep out of sight.

The sun struggled to escape from the clouds. Enough to melt the snow and cast a bit of greyish light. Still, it was cold. I forced myself to run down the hill, hoping no one would see me. But as it turned out, someone did. Someone who was watching me the entire time.

Chapter Nineteen: Ryn

*C*harlotte Campbell wasn't what I expected. She wasn't dowdy, bookish or nerdy, and I felt like a jerk for even conjuring up the stereotypical Classics scholar. I mean, after all, Linna was one, too, but Linna was hot long before she was scholarly.

I found Charlotte's building without too much trouble, just a long bus ride and an even longer walk around Harvard Yard until I spotted Boylston Hall. Finding her office was easier. The building had a directory.

"You must be Ryn," a voice called out from across a long, narrow room. "Come this way, my office is in here."

Charlotte Campbell apparently shared a suite of offices with other doctoral candidates who served as teaching assistants while they conducted their research. I could see a long, blond ponytail bobbing up and down as I followed her. She was tall, slender and drop-dead gorgeous. Had I known, I might have changed majors, transferred colleges and enrolled at Harvard. But lusting after language teachers never ends well. Long before

Linna, I fell for Mademoiselle Claudine in 8th grade. I wasn't about to let that happen again.

Charlotte Campbell pointed to two large chairs separated by a small coffee table.

"Sit down. Can I get you anything? Coffee? Water?"

"Thanks, no. I'm fine."

"So, you sounded urgent on the phone. And I'm more than curious. What could be so compelling about a 13th-century Scottish liturgy?"

"Maybe I will take some water, because it's a long story."

I handed Charlotte the printouts from the flash drive as well as the photocopies of the original parchment. Then I told her everything. The text, the secret encryptions, the fact that Linna thought someone was trying to murder the guy. All of it. All of it except the bit about time travel. Had I mentioned that particular nuance she would have called security. I just left it at Linna disappearing while she was translating the liturgy. Charlotte bought it.

"So you think her disappearance might have had something to do with this research?"

"Yeah, I mean, yes. Yes, I do. So can you help me? Can you translate this?"

Charlotte Campbell crinkled her nose and looked at the stack of papers. She leaned over to her desk and grabbed a pair of reading glasses. Like a model posing for a photo take, she started to sift through the papers.

"I have to admit, I'm intrigued. Intrigued, but concerned. You said your girlfriend was working on a government project?"

"My ex-girlfriend. Just friend. And it was a joint endeavor between the colleges and the government."

"Does anyone else know about this?"

"I don't think so. And no one knows that I came here to meet with you. I'm a bioengineering major at M.I.T., and believe me, no one there is the least bit interested in translating 13th-century Latin text."

Charlotte laughed and shook her head.

"Guess I've been watching too many espionage movies. Look, I'll tell you what. I'll translate this for you—at least the general idea. And I'll pay attention to the encrypted messages. But a project like this will take time. Give me a couple of weeks and I'll email you. Leave me your address."

She handed me a notepad and I scribbled my email and my cell number.

"I have to admit," she said. "This is fascinating. Maybe I should be working in Georgetown."

I stood up and placed the empty bottle of water on the coffee table.

"Thanks. This really means a lot to me."

"I can tell. She's a lucky ex."

Chapter Twenty:
Linna

At first it was just a soft buzz and I hardly noticed. Then it grew louder. All at once I was surrounded by bees, and lots of them. Instinctively, I started running faster, ignoring everything that I had been taught as a child. My heart was beating quicker than the speed of my legs as I ran down the slope. By now, I was totally surrounded and panic set in. I couldn't even scream for fear that the bees would get into my mouth. I tried to wave my shawl in the air, but that made things worse. Still, I kept running, numb with fear.

Suddenly, I heard someone calling out to me. I turned and with half-open eyes, looked straight at a young monk who was just a few feet away.

"Stepe! Stepe!"

I froze for just a second, long enough for him to place his hand over my nose and eyes and bend my head forward. Somehow I knew he wasn't trying to hurt me, just help me. I stayed still. He leaned over my back, tucking my head toward the ground. I was immobile. The seconds moved slowly. But the buzzing started to subside. Were the bees flying off? His hand was still covering my face. My eyes opened slowly just as he stepped back. The swarm had moved away.

I turned and faced the monk. He was standing so close to me that I could see the color of his eyes. Dark green. Straight jet-black hair framed his face, and I took a sharp breath. It wasn't as if I hadn't dated good-looking guys before. But this was different. Something deep and stormy about him, and I couldn't stop staring. Ryn was more than right. It was the stuff out of fairy tales. I was thunderstruck. The man took a step forward and lifted my chin. I felt as if every nerve in my body had gone haywire.

Stop it, Linna. Stop it!

In that instant, I got a good look at his hand. There was ink on his fingertips. Faded ink that had become embedded. It could only mean one thing. The man who prevented me from being stung by a swarm of bees was a scribe. And I was certain he was the one I had risked everything to find.

"Salvus?"

That was the only word in his sentence I understood. It was Latin. Something about being safe. I nodded. Then, he pointed to a small thatched roof lean-to that stood a few yards away. It held three rows of shelves and upside-down woven baskets. It took me a moment to grasp what I was looking at—an apiary. The woven baskets were hives and the monks were keeping bees for honey. But why would they attack?

The monk turned and faced the cloister that now stood above us. I could see a few other monks milling about the entryway. He said something else that I didn't understand, then turned and walked back uphill.

I don't know whatever possessed me, but I ran after him and grabbed his hand. Unable to say anything, I gave it a squeeze. And then, unexpectedly, he grinned. Subtle at first, then wider, revealing the most gorgeous smile I had ever seen.

I was thunderstruck all right. And no amount of rationalization or reasoning was going to change that.

Chapter Twenty-one: The Abbey, 1296

*B*rother Gregory had followed the precentor from the small burial preparation room to the outside passageway leading to the fields and apiary. He wondered why the monk who normally assisted with services had left the others so abruptly. In the darkened hallway adjacent to the corridor, he heard a voice that seemed to echo and resound. A voice in a place where all things should be silent. He heard the words, *"Later. After dark."* It had to be the precentor talking. But to whom? Stepping softly, he approached the monk unseen. And that's when he saw the girl.

Something about her looked familiar, but Brother Gregory couldn't quite grasp what it was. And why, of all things, was she in a place where lay people weren't permitted? He continued to approach them, but by the time he reached the end of the passageway, the precentor was no longer in sight and the girl was heading down the hill to the cottages below. He stood in the archway and watched her. Nothing unusual about local folk coming to the monastery to purchase breads or even sweet wine, but that kind of business was conducted openly, in the wooden kiosk near the cow pasture. One of the lay monks usually took care of that, certainly not the precentor.

A certain uneasiness crept over Brother Gregory, as if someone was trying to suffocate him with a veil. Quickly, he stepped out of the archway and into the open air. The girl was already partway down the knoll. Running and screaming. Her feet barely touched the ground. In a flash, the young monk knew exactly what had happened. Something or someone had disturbed the bees from the nearby apiary and they began to swarm the girl. If she kept running, she'd be stung over and over again.

The monk yelled for her to stop but she kept moving. He was too far away and she couldn't hear him. He ran, hardly noticing the rocks and ruts in the field as he caught up to her. Again, he yelled and this time she heard him, stopping long enough for him to cover her face and prevent her from antagonizing the already angered bees.

When the insects were no longer a threat, he paused and looked at her. Again, something familiar. He told her that she was safe and that she should return to the cottages below, but she just gazed at him.

At the moment when he turned to leave, she did the strangest thing. She grabbed his hand and held it. Long enough for him to feel a heat that was both unexpected and startling. Instinctively, he smiled. Then, without a word, he raced up the hill, darting back into the archway by the cloister.

Chapter Twenty-two:
Linna

I watched as the monk ran towards the archway, never turning around. It had to be mid-morning because the sky, although still greyish, began to lighten a bit even though the sun didn't break through the clouds. I started to walk down the slope. The cold and dampness made my body feel slow and clumsy, yet I could feel my heart pounding so fast that I had to remind myself to take deep breaths.

Relax, Linna. The bees aren't going to swarm you again. Unless that's not why your heart is racing.

I kept walking, turning back from time to time to look at the apiary. And then it dawned on me. Bees don't just leave their hives and swarm. Something had to spook them. Or maybe someone. All it would have taken was for a stone or two to be thrown at the beehives. But I wasn't a threat. Unless the swarm wasn't meant for me. Maybe someone knew that monk would run after me. And the bees would attack him. I stopped heading downhill and began to move parallel to where the hives were, remaining a good distance below them. From this vantage point I could see something that I hadn't noticed before. A few yards behind the dense trees that framed the apiary was another building, one that was partially hidden by the wooded area. Against the murky sky, thick white smoke was billowing out of a rounded tower at the edge of the structure. And the closer I got, the more intense the odor.

Be careful, Linna. They can see you now.

Acrid, pungent air seemed to fill my nostrils as I took a good look. I was standing below a complex of narrow buildings that connected to a tower. No wonder it wasn't visible before. It was built on the steep slope side of the monastery, and if I stayed well below it, only the top of my head could be seen.

As I crept closer, I could hear noise. Lots of noise. Pounding. Thudding. Scraping. Grinding. As the smoke got even more intense, it reminded me of the old basement furnace in my grandfather's house back in Cleveland. We used to visit there for the holidays when I was little. I pulled my shawl tighter and kept walking until I was just a few feet from the narrow building adjacent to the tower. Thankfully, no one was in sight.

The pounding noise was methodical—slow, deliberate and constant. As I approached, whatever heat was coming out of those buildings seemed to warm the air a bit. I wasn't as cold and my feet moved faster as I made a dash for the first archway. Pressing myself against the wall, I leaned in to take a look.

The interior of the tower was a huge round fireplace surrounded by men who were holding long pokers and prodding the contents in the fire. My face felt flushed with the heat as I watched them work and tried to process what I was seeing. Without warning, they stepped back and the air seemed to blast in a cloud that went straight up the chimney. In that split second, I knew immediately what it was—a forge. A blast furnace. Somehow, these monks were smelting iron.

My nostrils burned from the charcoal stench forcing me to lean back against the outside of the stone building. This was not what I had expected.

Well? What did you expect, Linna?

I had pictured a quaint little monastery in some secluded hills where the monks would be writing and praying all day. Sure, I figured they would have cows for milk and chickens for eggs, but I never envisioned anything like this. The abbey wasn't just an abbey. It was its own city—structured, complex and mysterious.

As the heat from the furnace continued to warm the air, I realized that I was just uncovering a small layer of its secrets.

Chapter Twenty-three:
Ryn

I had just flopped down on the couch when my phone buzzed. The MBTA in rush hour was worse than Logan Airport on Thanksgiving, but that's what you get when you schedule a meeting on a Friday afternoon at Harvard. I thought maybe Charlotte Campbell needed more information, but it was Aeden. I let out a slow breath. Did I really want to talk to her now or just let it go to voicemail? No doubt she was calling to remind me that Halloween was only a few weeks away.

The phone kept buzzing, and I knew I'd have to talk to her eventually, so I slid the arrow and said hello.

"Have you heard anything? Because I haven't and Mom would have called me. But that's not why I called. I have great news. The theater department is doing 'The Scottish Play' this spring and the costumes are getting re-sewn now."

"The Scottish play? What Scottish play? What costumes? What the heck are you talking about? And why should I be thrilled that your theater department is sewing clothes?"

"It's bad luck to say the name out loud. The play is cursed, you know. Okay, I'll whisper it. *Macbeth.* Shakespeare's tragedy."

I groaned, not because some play was cursed, but because I thought I'd have to sit through it. Aeden apparently didn't hear me or just ignored the groan because she kept talking.

"The play takes place in Scotland. In the Middle Ages. Okay, so maybe not the 13th century, but close enough. So that means I can get us clothes to wear if we… well, you know. If we decide to help Linna."

"Aeden, it's still way too soon for that. Besides, I'm kind of looking into something."

I then went on to tell her about the envelope and how Charlotte Campbell at Harvard agreed to translate the liturgies that Linna was working on.

"She might be able to give us more information. Information we might really need."

"Okay. But remember. We agreed. Halloween."

Then she said "bye" and I really groaned, because I didn't know what would be worse—trying to save an ex-girlfriend who was stuck on some dead monk or having to sit through a long and boring play. *Macbeth* wasn't cursed. I was.

Chapter Twenty-four: Linna

The pounding and grinding noises had stopped, replaced by a whooshing, bellowing sound. The heat, I imagine, working its way up the furnace. The crash of metal continued, only this time closer, beyond the corner of the building. It sounded as if someone was throwing heavy pieces of metal into something. Could that have scared the bees? Unlikely. Still, I was curious.

I moved slowly, still keeping myself pressed against the stone wall by the archway, until I was inches away from the edge of the building. I could see a wooden hay wagon a few feet away. The small spokes in its wheels were rough cut and uneven. Long pieces of black metal jutted up from the straw. Whatever was being forged by the monks working that furnace was getting loaded onto the wagon. I kept still and watched, hoping no one would look beyond the front of the building. A heavy-set man with reddish hair emerged from inside, carrying something in an old blanket or cloth. He moved quickly to the cart and added the contents to whatever was resting on the hay pile. Then he hurriedly covered it with the cloth and tossed straw all over it before returning to the forge.

"It could be anything," I thought. "Cranes, yokes for horses, even kettles." I figured they were getting ready to take the items into the nearest town for trade or barter. Nothing out of the ordinary. I watched as someone else approached the wagon. This time from the larger building on the other side of the tower. And instead of surveying the contents, this monk bent down underneath the chassis. I watched intently as he took something from his hand and started to cut the rope that held the wheels to the axle. If the cart couldn't pivot, it would topple over.

Oh my God! This guy is sabotaging whatever trade or sale is about to happen. But worse yet, when the cart tips over, it'll spook the plow horse and the driver is bound to fall. Unless that's the real intention. Is someone trying to kill more than my monk?

I held my breath and waited until I was sure the man had made it back to the large building. Whoever he was, I knew one thing. He wasn't acting alone. Someone had stabbed the old monk in the courtyard at dawn, and someone had angered the bees to attack the green-eyed monk, *my monk*. And now, this man had cut just enough rope to ensure that the driver would take a heavy fall. Too many incidents. It had to be more than one person. But why the cart? Unless someone wanted to make sure its contents never reached their destination. By now, I could feel my pulse racing.

I glanced quickly in both directions. No one was in sight. All I needed to do was to walk the few feet to the wagon, lift the cloth, and see what objects came out of that forge. With the shawl over my head, I bent down and made a quick dash to the spot, pulling back the thick muslin cloth so I could get a look at the objects. Too much straw on this side. I moved over to the edge of the cart that faced the woods and gave the cloth a shove. Then, I parted the straw from the pieces of metal to get a better look.

I gasped at what I saw. It was so unexpected. Before I had time to think, I heard the clank of more metal and the sound of footsteps coming down the hallway from the furnace to the archway. *Someone's adding to the load.*

Don't get caught, Linna. Do something.

By now I could feel my chest pounding and the adrenaline racing through my body. I don't remember ever feeling this way. The footsteps suddenly stopped, and I knew that someone was at the archway. My hands grabbed the wooden side of the cart and I hoisted myself inside, covering my body with the cloth.

Dumb move, Linna. He'll remove the cloth and he'll see you.

I held still. Waiting to be discovered. It was too late to do anything else. But no one came. The seconds turned to minutes and I started to breathe again. Slowly, I peered out from under the cloth. No sign of life except for the pounding noises coming from the furnace.

There had to be a way that I could tell someone about the frayed rope under the wagon. But I couldn't take that risk. Not now. I already had an invitation to another "game of chance," and I intended to take it. *Later. After dark.*

I sat up and lifted a leg over the edge of the wagon. Slowly. Carefully, so as not to topple over. When both of my feet were on the ground, I grabbed the cloth and rolled it up as if I were back in Girl Scout Camp and had to make a bedroll for one of our merit badges. The cloth was narrow enough to be tied to the rope underneath the wagon. Someone would see it! I left enough of it in plain sight. And once they untied it, they'd see that the rope had been cut.

Then, I thought about the contents of that wagon. Was I really making the right choice? Until I knew what was really happening I couldn't just walk away knowing someone was about to get hurt. I bit my lip and thought for a moment. Everything was becoming more complicated. All I wanted to do was to warn my monk ahead of time that his life was in danger. Maybe he'd leave the monastery. Maybe he'd… *What, Linna? Go back to the 21st century with you? Or were you planning to spend the rest of your life in the Middle Ages?* I didn't want to think about it any further because it was ludicrous. Ludicrous and stupid. Still, I couldn't stop thinking about him. He was no longer a scribe and a poet on paper. He was the man with the deep green eyes who pressed his body so close to mine that for a moment, our breath seemed to be coming from the same lungs.

He didn't want you to get stung by bees, Linna. Wake up!

I rubbed my hands together and started down the hill. Judging from the muted sunlight behind the clouds, it was early afternoon. I was cold, tired, and most of all, hungry.

There were barns and cottages below. All I needed to do was to get inside one of them and look for food. At nightfall I could make my way back to the abbey. The old, haggard monk in the passageway expected me. His words were clear and succinct.

"Later. After dark."

But who was he really expecting and what would happen if we both showed up?

Chapter Twenty-five:
The Abbey, 1296

*B*rother Gregory looked over his shoulder as the girl ambled down the hill. He had first spotted her in the hallway with Brother Alban, the abbey's precentor. Who the girl was, or why she was even in the cloister troubled him. Like so many other things as of late. She had to be one of the local girls from the cottages below that made up the small town below the berm that separated the abbey from the rest of the valley.

Still, something didn't seem right and that's why he followed her. Then, the bees. Swarming. Ready to attack. They'd never done anything like that in all the time that Brother Gregory had walked through the fields past the apiary. He had no choice, placing his own body over hers so she wouldn't get stung. Why then, did it feel as if a different kind of sting had taken over his hand? The hand that she held in such a tight grip that he could almost feel her pulse.

Shaking his head, he passed through the archway and continued down the hall until he reached the small washroom near the sanctuary. The monks had finished cleansing Brother Trewyn's body and had taken him to the area of repose awaiting burial and the special prayer ceremony.

The second death in such a short time. Brother Gregory saw the small puncture wound in the monk's neck. Had the others noticed it as well? If so, no one uttered a word or made a sign. No one dared to mouth the unmentionable—murder.

The first was Brother Jarvin. He had died less than a fortnight ago. Old age. Natural causes. But there was nothing natural about a slow poisoning. Again, had anyone noticed the tremor in his hands or the fact that his skin had taken on a greyish pallor? If so, they remained silent.

The abbey, once a place of solace for Brother Gregory, had now become claustrophobic. He felt trapped and constricted. Walking slowly, he looked down at his hand. It was as if he could feel that girl's palm in his. Smooth, soft, and cold. She had probably just reached out to thank him, but he knew otherwise. He saw the look in her face. It was as if she were trying to tell him something but couldn't.

Her lips had parted slightly, as he waited for a word or two to slip from her mouth, but nothing. All she could do was stare. It was impossible for him to not notice her wide brown eyes. Or the reddish blush on her face after narrowly escaping the bees.

Brother Gregory closed his hand and placed the other one over it as he continued down the hallway.

What he wanted to write and what he needed to say were not the words found in a liturgy. It would be a long afternoon in the little room with the other silent scribes. But he knew the girl would be back that night. He had heard the precentor's demand as well.

"Later. After dark."

And while the bees would no longer pose a threat, the young monk began to wonder if something far more dangerous awaited that girl. He swore he could still feel her skin against his palm. And one thing was certain. He, too, would be waiting in the corridor by the cloister after dark.

Chapter Twenty-six: The Abbey, 1296

It was early afternoon. The red-haired monk wiped the sweat from his brow as he headed back to the forge. He hoped the extra weight in the wagon wouldn't be too much for the horse when it pulled the cart the next day. Villagers were expecting pots, tins and cauldrons. King Edward's men were expecting something else.

As he started to step into the archway that led to the furnace, he thought he caught a glimpse of some movement near the trees. Turning abruptly he walked back to the cart and stood still. No sounds. No movement. Everything was just as he left it minutes ago.

"Just the wind," he imagined, "moving the tree limbs about." He held his breath. Brother Rulf had that strange sensation that he was being watched. Still, there was no reason for alarm. He walked back to the forge and took his spot near the bellows. Yet something wasn't right. Each push of air seemed to emit an alarm that pulsated through him. Brother Rulf was now certain that it wasn't the wind that had disturbed the branches. He twisted his neck and stretched his arms, pretending that he needed to take a break. Quickly, he headed back to the wagon, if nothing else than to convince himself that it was just a cloud of dark thoughts that had gotten into his mind. But as soon as he approached the clearing by the trees, he knew otherwise. Everything had been disturbed.

The straw had been moved and the cart seemed to tilt. Brother Rulf took a closer look and stared at the undercarriage. The piece of cloth that he had used when he loaded the wagon was now underneath it. He bent down and took a closer look. The rope that held the wheels to the axle had been cut! If that wasn't enough, whoever did the deed bragged and boasted by tying the cloth to the chassis. Their message was clear and succinct. *King Edward will have to wait another day for his goods.*

Whoever had done this must have been watching Brother Rulf closely. But who? None of the monks who were working at the blast furnace left the forge. The nearest building was yards away down the path that led to the courtyard. Still… someone could have been hiding.

Brother Rulf pulled the cloth out from under the wagon. Hastily, he unloaded the contents from the cart onto the cloth and covered it with straw before turning the wagon over to fix the rope. The gash was deep and he would need to find new rope. That meant walking to the long building where fibers of hemp were twisted and braided to form the ropes they used to tie their robes and secure their wagons. If he hurried, he might be able to fix the wagon before he was expected for afternoon prayers.

Glancing down the hill as he strode towards the Ropewalk building, Brother Rulf saw the girl running to the cottages below. Her long brown skirt and black shawl swept across the berm like a dark omen. And in that instant, his thoughts turned even blacker.

Chapter Twenty-seven: Linna

The sun had just started to set when I made it back up the hill to the monastery unseen. I knew I'd have to reach the back of the cloister hall before it got dark. I had no lantern, no candle, nothing to guide me. As I got closer, I could hear the faint murmurs of the monks at prayer. The open archways from the sanctuary let the voices skim through the air like leaves caught up in the wind. I walked to the very spot where the old, gaunt monk had first seen me and leaned against the cold, stone wall. Darkness would come and so would he. At least I wasn't hungry.

I had managed to sneak into a barn where someone had left a crust of old honey bread, and I devoured it as if it had just come out of an oven. There were wooden buckets, too, with water for the animals, and I helped myself, trying not to think about where it had come from. But most of the time, I kept my distance behind the cottages watching as people went about their lives. It became clear that the cottages were their places of business, too. Bakers, cooks, candle and basket makers. I caught glimpses of all of them as I navigated around the town like some kind of thief. But if I was guilty of stealing anything, it was time. And I wasn't really stealing it. I was borrowing it.

I waited for what seemed like hours. The sun had set and a few stars dotted the horizon. I could no longer hear the voices from the church, and the silence seemed to have a roar of its own. I paced back and forth across the corridor, not knowing what to expect. And then, footsteps. Slow and steady footsteps. *He must be coming. That old monk is just a few yards away.* I stood at attention, pressing myself against the wall. But the footsteps stopped. Almost as if someone decided not to walk any further. I took a deep breath and exhaled slowly. My hands were shaking and I could feel my heart speeding up. *Maybe this wasn't such a good idea, Linna.* Before I had time to think, I saw a faint light at the end of hallway. The footsteps had resumed. I held still and waited until I could see the monk's features, illuminated grotesquely by the dim light of the flickering candle that he held in one hand. Tucked under his other arm was something wrapped in cloth.

Suddenly, the man pressed the object into my stomach, catching me off guard. I grabbed it before it dropped to the ground. Then, he spoke.

"*Snyre!*"

It was Old English, or Gaelic. At first my mind couldn't process it. I was lost. I froze. But only for a second, and that's when everything seemed to click in my mind. *For Heaven's sake, Linna, he's a monk. He knows Latin. Don't just stand there. Speak back in Latin!*

I whispered back.

"Quid vis?"

Before he had the chance to reply, a clanging sound reverberated in the passageway, as if someone further down that hall had dropped something. The echo was fickle and I had no way of knowing which direction the sound had come from. Apparently, it was enough of a warning, because the monk quickly blew out the candle and distanced himself from the spot where we were standing.

He knew the passageway. In all of his years in the abbey he had probably memorized every stone and every step in the hall. He had the advantage. I was left in the darkness. Not knowing what I was holding or what I was supposed to do. I didn't realize that in an instant, everything would change.

Chapter Twenty-eight:
The Abbey, 1296

*B*rother Alban knew without hesitation that he had been followed. He quickly turned from the girl and headed back to the small alcove by the sanctuary. Whoever had followed him here could still be waiting, and Brother Alban was not about to risk an encounter. Not here. Not now. A strong sense of dread lingered over him as he moved in the darkness through the passageway. He slowed his steps and glided his hand against the wall. Few monks knew of the hidden opening to the sanctuary, but Brother Alban did. It was where he had hidden the reliquary. He bent down to the ground and crawled carefully under a small archway into another hallway. It ran parallel to the main passage and had been built as a hiding place should the abbey ever be attacked. Once there, Brother Alban let out a slow breath and turned his thoughts back to the girl. Something was amiss, but he couldn't explain it.

That girl knew what to do. Why then was she acting so strange? It wasn't as if this were the first time she had met with him to secure a reliquary and take it to her father. The old man knew that King John's army would pay a dear price for it. Brother Alban was counting on that. But it was the Latin that unnerved him most of all. The girl spoke Latin. Blasphemy! It was the language of the church, not the village.

In a matter of minutes Brother Alban had reached the alcove adjacent to the sanctuary. He took a deep breath and entered slowly, comforted by the silence and stillness in the church. By now the other monks had gathered for the Compline service. He would need to lead the prayers as he always did—intent and devote. More so, he would need to clear his mind of the girl. It was done. She had the reliquary. In a few weeks' time, the abbey would reap the bounty. It was a matter of survival. Even if it meant going against every core belief in order to ensure that the abbey remain standing. As for the man who followed him… that would wait till another day.

The precentor had gotten word that King John Balliol would pay a hefty fee for the reliquary, a small piece of cheekbone from the apostle James, son of Zebedee. However, the bone that they held was from a slaughtered ox, aged and fashioned carefully. Brother Alban and Brother Trewyn had seen to that. Brother Jarvin as well. The precentor shuddered to think that their deaths had anything to do with the clandestine hoax. Besides, didn't the infirmarian say that Brother Jarvin died of old age? Still, Brother Alban felt uneasy.

He walked quietly to the altar and nodded at the sacrist before uttering the opening prayer. A few yards away in the hallway, there were other utterances. But no one heard those.

Chapter Twenty-nine:
Linna

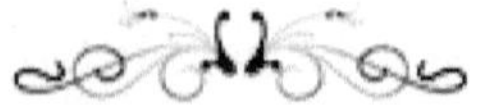

I stood motionless in the hallway, my arms wrapped tightly around the object that was concealed in cloth. Careful, so as not to drop it, I undid a fold in the material and reached my hand inside to see what it was. As soon as my fingers touched the surface, I could feel the indentations on wood. The box! I was holding a reliquary. And a fake one at that! Contained in an ornate box to make it look as if it was valuable. Fabricating reliquaries was the dirty deed that the old monks perpetuated in the dead of night under the monastery.

Immediately, I understood. That haggard monk mistook me for the go-between. The one who would sell the fake reliquary that I was holding. Why would they do such a thing? Wasn't the monastery self-sufficient? That's what we were taught in elementary social studies. Then again, we were taught so many things that I continue to question today. Yet the biggest question of all was, "What on earth should I do?"

The truth of the matter was that I needed to get back into the abbey and warn my monk. And if someone expected me after dark, then no one would question me. But it wasn't exactly an invitation. More like a summons and dismissal all at once. *Great going, Linna. Now what?* I knew that the monks were all in the church for the evening prayer. All I had to do was to sneak across the courtyard and wait for the one with the green eyes. I'd find a way to get his attention. Maybe toss a small pebble in his path.

He had to be warned now, before it was too late. The plan to murder him was already in motion when he encrypted it into the liturgy. Only that would be weeks from now. He still had a chance to leave. *If* I could convince him.

It was pitch black in the cloister corridor and the only way I could walk was to run my hand along the stone wall, inching slowly until it led to the open courtyard. The moon and night sky would give me enough light once I got there.

I tried to cushion my footsteps as I walked. After a few yards, it seemed to get easier. Maybe my eyes were getting acclimated to the darkness because it didn't seem as black. Then I realized that a faint light was being cast behind me, but just as I started to turn around, someone grabbed a handful of hair from the back of my head, gave me a shove and yelled.

"Thēof!"

I tightened my grip on the box and used my free hand to lash out at whoever called me a thief. In the flickering light, I could see it was a girl. A girl who looked so much like me that I was momentarily stunned. She backed away, afraid of dropping the candle she was holding. And when her eyes met mine, I could see the shock on her face as well.

So this was whom the old monk expected.
 In the scant light, I tried to get a better look. Was this the girl from the cottage that first night when I arrived back in time? Her hair was longer, slightly below shoulder length and her cheeks were a bit fuller. But the eyes, the brow, the nose and the mouth were the same features I had seen in the mirror for over eighteen years.

I was about to respond with a "Thēof Nay!" when I heard the pounding of footsteps headed our way. The girl froze for an instant, then motioned for me to follow and ran down the passageway. We slipped past the open arch and sank into the thick grass that covered the berm before heading downhill. Me, holding the reliquary, and my mirror image waving a thin tapered candle against the night sky. Neither of us turned to see whose footsteps they were. It was just as well.

Chapter Thirty:
The Abbey, 1296

Brother Gregory wedged himself into the narrow crawlspace adjacent to the alcove in the cloister corridor. He had to move quickly because the footsteps were right behind him. Someone else was following Brother Alban. Did they know about the girl as well? Brother Gregory held still. He remembered hearing Brother Alban's voice just the other day and it had jarred him. He had only heard the man speak Latin during the prayer services but this time he was speaking another tongue—the common language. It was just one word—*snyre.* And it was meant for the girl. He wanted her to hurry. Now he was about to hear that voice again.

For weeks now, Brother Gregory had suspected the precentor of something sinister, but it was just a feeling, a suspicion. Until that night when the light from a flickering candle lead him to the labyrinth below the wine cellar. Brothers Alban and Trewyn were holding something. A box perhaps? That much he could see before the candle went out. And then he had to run in the darkness up the stairs until he reached the wine cellar and could exit into the courtyard.

The young monk began to question everything. Why did Brother Alban leave the lavatorium when the others were preparing Brother Trewyn's body? As precentor, Brother Alban should have stayed. Instead, he had words with the dark-eyed girl and told her to return after dusk. Something wasn't right, and that's why Brother Gregory decided to slip quietly from the procession leading into the Compline service and see for himself what Brother Alban had intended for the girl.

He had barely started to walk when he heard footsteps behind him. Brother Gregory could not let himself be seen. He held his breath in the semi-darkness and waited for the man to pass directly in front of him. What he didn't expect was for the monk to thunder past him, taking such long strides that Brother Gregory couldn't determine who it was, only that this monk was extremely large. A formidable presence like so many of the others who worked in the grange, the kitchen or the forge.

The sound of those footsteps ceased in an instant. That could only mean one thing. The man was standing still, waiting. The silence seemed to stretch for an eternity. Still, Brother Gregory refused to move.

Without warning, the footsteps resumed. Louder. Heavier. Faster. Brother Gregory took a breath and followed the sound. Was it the girl this man was after or Brother Alban? And would there be another murder tonight?

Chapter Thirty-one:
Linna

I tried to move quickly in the stinging night air, but the grass below my feet was tall and it felt as if each blade was trying to pull me to the ground. Still, I kept running downhill. The girl was a few feet ahead of me and she kept yelling to me. My eyes burned as I strained to see her in the semi-darkness. With the exception of some faint starlight and the dim sliver of the moon against the clouds, it was impossible to see anything clearly. There were torch lights scattered among the cottages, but I had no way of gauging the distance between me and the town below.

The small reliquary box was still tucked under my arm, concealed in cloth. Although I was no thief, I was holding something that wasn't mine. For some reason, I gripped it tighter and kept running downhill, my feet gliding on the slippery grass that I imagined was always wet this time of year from the light snow. The girl was moving faster as if she knew we had a reason to be afraid. And then, the worst! I tripped and plunged headfirst onto the ground. The box clipped the side of my jaw and the pain seared through me as if someone delivered a knockout punch. I could feel the tears welling up in my eyes just as the girl took a step towards me.

"Astandan! Snyre!"

It sounded like she was telling me to stand up. She kept getting louder as I crawled on my knees with the reliquary pressed against my stomach and stumbled to get up. Even in the dark I could see the fear on her face. Someone was behind us. Someone was getting closer.

I tried to take a step forward when another kind of pain made my entire body cringe. My ankle. I had twisted my ankle. The girl watched as I took small clumsy steps towards her.

"Snyre!"

She motioned for me to keep moving, but instead I held the box out to her. She needed it. Not me.

"Yours!" I said, hoping that the word bore some resemblance to the Old English/Gaelic she spoke.

Her hands moved tentatively at first as if she expected me to grab her or even kick her. I shoved the reliquary towards her and let go, watching as she draped the cloth around it and started heading downhill. Again she said the same word—*snyre*. The old monk had used it as well. But there was no way I could keep up with her. I motioned for her to keep going and then I sank back down in the grass, hoping that whoever was following us didn't get a good look below the berm.

I could hear the sound of a faint wind and some rustling from the woods. *It's only deer, Linna. Night animals. Just stay still.* Whoever was lurking behind me never approached any further. I reasoned that it was the reliquary they wanted, not me. Still, I waited until the partial moon moved a good distance in the sky before standing up. My ankle hurt, but not badly enough to prevent me from walking. My body was cold and numb. I never expected this. *What did you expect Linna?*

Slowly, I made my way back up the hill. There was no reason for me to return to the small enclave where the girl lived. Except perhaps to steal food, and I was doing a decent job of that at the monastery. Besides, I had to return to the abbey. My monk had to be warned. It wasn't safe for him to stay. In that instant, I knew exactly what I needed to do. It couldn't wait. It had to be done while there was still enough moonlight for me to find my way.

My body shook in the night cold as I crept closer to the outer wall of the monastery. Funny, but I thought I heard Ryn's voice. *"It's always cold in Scotland."*

Each step I took seemed to get louder as I made my way back. This time I circumvented the cloister and entered the courtyard through the path that linked it to the forge. If there were monks hiding behind the archways or alcoves, they knew how to keep their silence and they knew how to protect their secrets.

Chapter Thirty-two:
The Abbey, 1296

*B*rother Gregory carefully calculated the distance of the footsteps as the intensity of their sound began to wane. When he was certain the large monk had neared the archway that opened to the hill and apiary, he slowly inched his way forward in the dark. He expected the men to be standing over the berm. He also expected the dark-eyed girl to be there as well. But as Brother Gregory approached, all he could see was darkness. There was no sign of Brother Alban or the others.

He stepped out of the cloister corridor and let his eyes adjust to the darkness. Below him he could see the large monk running past the apiary toward the cluster of cottages below. If that monk was after the girl, she was well out of reach. Probably nearing the cottages by now. But where was Brother Alban? He wasn't on the hill or in the hallway. Unless he knew another way back to the sanctuary. Whatever secret was between Brother Alban and the girl, this was neither the time nor the place for Brother Gregory to find out. He had more to fear from the heavy-set monk who would be returning from his useless chase after the girl. If only Brother Gregory had gotten a better look at the man, but the young scribe couldn't risk being seen. He took a deep breath and hurried back to the Compline service, entering unobtrusively, with his head bowed down in solemn reflection.

It was only when he lifted his eyes at the end of the prayer service did he see the precentor, Brother Alban, standing directly in front of the dais as the sacrist rang the small bronze bell. Row by row, the monks filed out and walked slowly across the courtyard to the dormitories.

From the narrow window at the top of the stairs Brother Gregory could see the figure of the large monk returning from below the hill. As the man passed by the torch on the side of the garden wall, his bright red hair looked as if it were a ring of fire. In that instant, Brother Gregory knew where he had seen that monk before. The forge. Working the blast furnace to cast metal, shaping vessels, instruments and utensils for prayer.

Brother Gregory had eyed the laborers during his allotted time for solace and reflection. They were brothers, yes, but they were *conversi*. They had taken the vows, but were not bound to the rigid prayer and devotion as were the others in his order. They were the farmers, the masons, and the iron workers. One foot in the physical world, the other in the spiritual.

For Brother Gregory, it was all about devotion. He had come to the abbey as a young boy. The second son of a noble family. Well educated in Latin and mathematics. His father had paid the abbey dearly in bullion and land so that his son would be shielded from any uprisings resulting from the death of Alexander III. Brother Gregory's path to salvation was in the scriptorium, where inkpots and parchment became manuscripts and liturgies. And unlike the *conversi,* his feet were planted in the spiritual world. It was only when the dark-eyed girl grasped his hand that he began to question his world.

He shivered slightly as he watched the red-haired monk return to the dormitory. The girl was safe for the moment. Back in her cottage. But Brother Gregory knew she would return. And this time it might not be the red-haired monk she would have to outrun.

Chapter Thirty-three: Linna

*I*t was that awful time when night is almost over but daybreak seems as if it will never come. The moon had slipped to the horizon and the light from the stars had gotten dimmer. No more night sounds. Whatever animals prowled for prey had long been satiated. I had made it through the courtyard and up the narrow stairs that led to the small room where the scribes spent their days. No one would be entering this room until mid-morning. Plenty of time for me to warn my monk and escape without notice.

The smell of ink seemed to overtake the room. Deep. Almost chemical. Funny, but for just a second it reminded me of a different chemical smell—the dry erase markers on the whiteboards in my high school. I took slow steps as I entered. In a little while the sun would be up and there would be enough light for me to study the parchments on each of the small tables. I would recognize mine. Or should I say *his*? And then, I would know exactly where to leave my message.

I'd never used a quill before or an inkpot for that matter, but if I took my time, I was sure I could spell out the one sentence that he had to see.

De monasterio exire! Non es securus.

The ink dripped on the first piece of parchment and I pushed it off to the side of the table where I had decided to sit. *Damn it all! This is going to take me much longer than I expected.* I was more careful the second time, doling out the ink as if it were an elixir. Then, while I waited for it to dry, I went from table to table, making absolutely certain that nothing was disturbed as I lifted each piece of parchment and studied the writing. Some I could dismiss immediately. They were illustrations or verses for chants. Others took me longer. By now the sun had come up at full strength and it had almost peaked in the sky. Noon. The monks would offer prayers, dine, and then begin their assigned tasks. I had to hurry. Only three more tables to go.

The first was a long biblical commentary about Genesis. *Move on, Linna. Not your monk.* Only two tables to go. I reached for the parchment that was resting on the nearest table and was just about to read it when the prayer bell chimed and I jumped, bumping into the table and knocking over a larger scroll of parchment that was off to the side. Quickly, I went to reposition it when I noticed something familiar. The shape of the lowercase letter R. That funny spacing and the way it looked like a v that was off kilter. I'd seen it before. There was no mistaking it. This was my monk's table and these were his works.

I put the rolled parchment back in its place and hid my message underneath it. By this afternoon he would know that he was no longer safe in the monastery and that he had to find a way out. But would he leave? Somehow, I had to make sure of that and the only way I knew how was to threaten the daylights out of him. I needed to write another message and I needed to write it fast.

Hurrying, I grabbed the piece of parchment that had the spilled ink and this time I used my words well.

Sanguis tuus privabitur—It's just ink this time. Next time it will be your blood.

Chapter Thirty-four: Linna

The chimes rang out just as I replaced the quill in the inkpot. Mid-day. I was exhausted from lack of sleep, but thankfully, I wasn't thirsty or hungry. I had managed to find my way into the kitchen when everyone was asleep last night and gorged myself on apples and dry bread. I even found pitchers of sweet tasting liquid that helped to wash everything down. Now all I had to do was to wait. Wait for my monk to read the message and leave the monastery. I knew that if he were to stay here any longer he'd uncover something far worse than those monks selling fake reliquaries. He'd learn what they were really smelting in the forge. Moreover, that knowledge would get him killed.

I had to make sure he left this abbey before it was too late. Why on earth did I feel as if it wasn't enough? As if I needed to be with him? It was a feeling I couldn't shake no matter how I tried to rationalize things. Then there was Ryn. For some inexplicable reason, I kept hearing his voice in my head.

"I don't know what's worse, Linna. The fact that he's dead or the fact that he's a monk?" I answered him out loud without even realizing it.

"Yeah, well, men joined the monasteries for all sorts of reasons back then. Maybe his had nothing to do with religion."

"Nice try, Linna. Maybe the Pope took office because he liked the view from the Vatican!"

The last chime sounded and I had to move quickly in spite of my sore ankle. *Athletes walk the pain off after an injury. So can you, Linna.* I could see the monks crossing the courtyard and heading to their duties. The scribes would be here in a matter of minutes. I made it to the stairwell and down the narrow steps through an archway that opened into a small inner garden. Its walls were low enough for me to scale without needing a boost. *Forget the pain, Linna. Use your good leg.* Ankle or no ankle, the thick brambles that surrounded the wall were another story. I scanned the perimeter looking for any kind of clearing. No luck. I covered my hands with the ends of the shawl so my fingers wouldn't get cut and then I hoisted myself over the wall. It was tougher than getting into that wagon. At least the cart had a lip edge and a soft landing. This had nothing. I fell onto the hard ground, aggravating the ankle that I had already twisted.

Directly in front of me was a small potter's shed. It looked like it had been vacant for a long time. The low stool that sat in the middle of the floor looked anything but inviting. Still, it was all I had, and I desperately needed some sleep. Just an hour or so until the scribes were done with their afternoon tasks. Then, I would find a way back to the courtyard unseen. From there to the cloister corridor and down the hill to the cottages and the road. I'd watch for my monk with the green eyes and follow him. I knew once he read my notes he would get out of here.

As it turned out, I could not have been more wrong.

Chapter Thirty-five:
The Abbey, 1296

It was just a quick gesture from the wrist but Brother Rulf knew its intent. From across the long wooden supper table someone gave him a message that needed no words. Brother Rulf bent his head down revealing the flaming crown that gave him the moniker of "red-haired monk." He rested the palm of his hand on his plate, signaling that he was ready for information. Then, he watched as the monk seated on the other side of the room placed his index finger on the edge of the table and tapped it twice before turning his head to face the side of the room closest to the hill. Brother Rulf understood.

Brother Alban would be heading down the corridor towards the hill tonight.

The monk from across the room slid his hand over the empty plate and stared directly at Brother Rulf. No further explanation was needed. The red-haired monk knew that he alone would have to confront the precentor tonight. No other time. It had to be prior to the Compline service.

What he didn't know was that Brother Alban had arranged for another meeting. One with a dark-eyed girl who lived in one of the cottages below. A girl who was no stranger to the secrets of the abbey.

Brother Rulf stepped back from his usual place in the processional, pretending to nurse a sore knee. He walked steadily through the garden path around the outside cloister until he reached the archway that led down a long corridor to the hill below the monastery. He had to hurry. Brother Alban was probably facing the hill by now. With all the speed he could muster, the red-haired monk took off running as he slammed his heels into the stone floor, narrowly missing Brother Gregory who was just inches from him, wedged into a small dark alcove.

The red-haired monk forced his tired body to keep running until he reached the archway that opened onto the hill. No sign of Brother Alban. Had the other monk lied to him? It seemed unlikely. Brother Rulf stepped outside and looked down at the hill. He couldn't believe what he was seeing. That same girl, the one who had severed the rope to the wagon, was running down the hill. Someone was in front of her, but it was too dark to see.

Without wasting a second, Brother Rulf charged toward the girl. She was only a few yards away. But the berm was steep and within minutes, everything turned to shadows. He stopped for a moment, waiting for something to move. It was as if the girl had vanished into the night air.

In the distance he heard the last chime of the night. The Compline service had ended. Without hesitation, Brother Rulf turned from the hill and started back to the courtyard, hoping the shadows would hide him as well.

Chapter Thirty-six:
The Scriptorium

The mid-day chime had ended and the scribe turned his attention to the inkpot at his table. He didn't remember leaving the quill adjacent to it. His eyes glanced at the sheets of parchment to his left. There should only have been one—the liturgy he was composing. Slowly, so as not to call attention to himself, the scribe lifted the parchment paper. He could feel the blood draining from his face as soon as he read the message.

Leaning over the table with his head facing down, the monk turned his eyes to both sides of the room. He could see the old monks, who had mastered their craft decades ago, inscribing liturgies and prayers. There were only a handful of younger scribes like him. Most of them came to the abbey as oblates who were turned over to the church by their noble families. He was not one of those.

His eyes moved slowly, lingering at each table before reading the message again. He knew that whoever had written it was not one of the men in the room. Although the Latin was precise, the script was choppy and hesitant. As if its author had more to fear than the reader. Or maybe they were just in a hurry. The scribe stood up and walked to the long table where the inkpots were stored. Whoever had written the note had never learned how to use the ink sparingly.

The monk's hands trembled slightly as he poured the fresh ink into his pot. So someone knew. He supposed it was Brother Alban, the unofficial head of the triumvirate. But if anyone should fear anything, it should be Brother Alban, because the other two monks who shared his authority were dead. Brother Jarvin weeks ago, and most recently Brother Trewyn. Still, the scribe knew a warning when he saw one. He would have to act now, before Brother Alban had the chance to select two new men to present to the abbot.

He eyed the scribe sitting next to him as he stood up to return the inkpot. No one suspected anything and that's how it had to be.

Chapter Thirty-seven:
Ryn

I had forgotten that I had put my phone on "mute" before I went to bed. I wanted to get a decent night's sleep without wrong numbers, butt calls from friends who had me on speed dial, or my sister who kept reminding me that Halloween was getting closer. Like I couldn't figure that out from looking at a calendar.

It was only when I took a seat in my biological engineering design class that I realized I hadn't received any text messages or calls that morning. The instructor hadn't arrived yet, so I quickly took out my phone and changed the setting to vibrate. Then, I scanned for messages. Aeden. What else was new? Reminder for a dental cleaning tomorrow. They better not find a damn cavity. Two texts from the guys at the lab about getting together over the weekend and a voicemail from Charlotte Campbell.

I immediately listened to her message.

"I'm not through with the translation yet, Ryn, but I think there's something you should know. The monk who wrote this was amazingly clever. There were

hidden messages within the first set of encryptions. Call me."

I glanced at the analog clock on the wall. The lecture would begin in seven minutes. *Maybe.* No sign of the instructor. I pushed the send button and waited for Charlotte to pick up.

"Ryn," her voice sounded alarmed. *"I was waiting for your call."*

"Yeah, sorry about that. I just got to my messages. What did you find out?"

"Your former girlfriend was right. There were layers of coded secret messages. I haven't seen anything like this since I studied the old Kabbalistic prayers. What I need to tell you is that she only figured out a small piece of this complex puzzle. And I'm far from being done myself. At this point, I don't have any reason to believe that her disappearance had anything to do with this translation. Then again, I might uncover something else as I keep going. The scribe who wrote this was tricky."

"What do you mean?"

"He used layers of innuendos and double entendre. Very sophisticated Latin, even for a monk. But that's not why I called you."

"Then, why?"

"Ryn, the monk who wrote this is not about to be murdered. He's the killer."

I almost dropped the phone.

"Are you still there? Did you hear what I said?"

"Yeah, I did."

Charlotte continued to talk. Something about getting back to me with more information. I said thanks and slipped my phone into my pocket just as the instructor walked to the podium. He dimmed the lights and turned on the computer. Across the large screen in the front of the room were the words "Integration of Biochemistry, Biology and Engineering." The instructor started droning on about the need for all disciplines to share information, but all I heard were Charlotte Campbell's words, *"Ryn, he's not about to be murdered. He's the killer."*

Part Two:

More Murders

Chapter Thirty-eight:
The Abbey, 1296

As he passed the tall narrow window to the right of the stairwell, Brother Gregory looked at the courtyard by the Garth, an old walled garden once cultivated for its herbs. He could see the potting shed, and in the distance, someone walking in the direction of the forge. He paused for a moment to take a better look. It was the girl. The dark-eyed girl. Brother Gregory could feel his heartbeat quicken as he moved down the stairs.

Forcing himself to turn away, he clenched his fists and proceeded to the church. He needed time to think and most of all, time to pray. Everything seemed to be closing in on him, but most frightening of all was how he felt when he saw her. As if she was lifting a veil into the sunlight to obliterate his darkest thoughts.

He moved steadily across the path in the long file of monks, pausing only once to glance over the stone wall. In the distance he could see the forge and the girl's silhouette. This time she wasn't alone. Someone either followed her or had intended to meet her. Brother Gregory couldn't be sure. But later, when he realized that Brother Alban was not conducting the Nones prayers, the young monk's thoughts began to spin out of control. Brother Alban always conducted the ninth hour prayers as well as the morning services, Vespers, and the Compline prayers. He had to be the one standing near the forge with the dark-eyed girl.

It was easy for Brother Gregory to slip out the door as he had done before. But this time, instead of a winding cloister corridor, he took the courtyard path to the old herb garden and then to the forge.

Smoke and soot filled the sky as he got closer to the furnace. The fire had recently been extinguished for the day and its remnants clung to the air, refusing to let go. The young scribe started to take longer strides until he could see the archway to the chimney tower. But the dark-eyed girl was nowhere in sight and neither was Brother Alban.

Still, the young monk approached the furnace. As he got closer, the smell from whatever metal had been forged seemed tainted and foul. In an instant, Brother Gregory knew what his nostrils were inhaling and he started to gag. It was the smell of burnt hair. And burnt flesh. His eyes saw what his mind tried to comprehend. Brother Alban's outer robe and vestments were torn and piled in a heap next to the chimney.

Sludge pots were tossed about the floor along with broken shards of pottery. Whoever struggled with Brother Alban had to be strong enough to overcome him and clever enough to lure him to this place. And what better way than to use the dark-eyed girl.

His mind raced as he struggled to make sense of it. Brother Alban was dead and the girl was nowhere in sight. Like the hive on the hill, the abbey had been disturbed, and this time the girl would have more to fear than bees.

Chapter Thirty-nine:
Ryn

Damn it, Linna. It was bad enough you lost it over some dead monk, but it turns out you're trying to save the wrong guy. What do you plan to do next? Create a database for Jack the Ripper?

I knew I was getting unhinged. Ex-girlfriends will do that to you. But Linna was in *way* over her head and I didn't have time to wait for Halloween and my deal with Aeden. *Aeden.* I got exhausted just thinking about it. It would be hard enough getting Linna the hell out of there, but having to contend with my sister gave it a whole new dimension.

Aeden would get side tracked. She always does. And it would just mess things up. But how the heck could I tell her that this was one time when I needed to go back alone? She'd freak-out and carry a grudge. The kind of stuff you watch on Dr. Phil. Hell, I could see the TV listing now. *"Brother betrays sister. Can she ever forgive him?"*

My stomach started to tighten up as I reached for my phone. I had to call her. What the heck. Years of family analysis might be a good thing. I slid the arrow and saw the message. Voicemail. Aeden's voicemail.

Terrific. I figured I'd play it and then get to feel really rotten and guilty. As things turned out, it was Aeden who got to feel that way.

"Don't be pissed, Ryn. Just listen. Maria Menounos is coming here for Halloween. She graduated in 2000 from Emerson. And I'm going to be escorting her to all of the theater events. Do you know what a big deal this is? What a big deal she is? The chance to be with a famous celebrity doesn't just drop in your lap. And she's famous—'Access Hollywood,' 'Today,' 'Extra.' I don't blame you if you never speak to me again, but honestly Ryn, I wouldn't stand in your way if some famous biology-engineering celeb walked into your life. Call me. Better yet—text me."

I texted her all right.

"Maria who?"

Yeah, I know I should have felt relieved. It was what I wanted after all. Still, I felt annoyed. Maybe we did need Dr. Phil. Then I remembered something about *Macbeth* and Scottish clothes. I didn't have time for all of that. Besides, every costume shop in Cambridge was doing a landmark business this week with frat parties, Halloween parties, zombie parties and every other reason to go berserk in October. I planned to do it as a monk. Until I realized it would never work. I didn't have that whole pious thing down and besides, I had no idea what color robe to get. The Middle Ages had all sorts of monks—Blackfriars, Greyfriars, and the other ones that I couldn't remember from middle school social studies. So that left me with one other choice—to dress like someone at the end of the 13th century. Try that at your local costume store. It was a nightmare.

By the end of the day, I had purchased a ridiculous looking outfit from Boston Costume, right here on Broadway in Cambridge. The salesgirl, who couldn't have been older than sixteen, thought I was out of touch. *Yeah, well, you don't know the half of it.*

"Are you sure you don't want to look at our super heroes section? Or maybe the vampire and werewolf line?"

"No," I said, trying to keep my voice calm and reasonable. "I need something from the 13th century. Something medieval. Got anything like that?"

The girl sighed as if I'd asked her to inventory the entire place.

"I'll go look. I think I remember seeing that stuff last summer when someone needed to rent it for the Renaissance Festival. Is that what you're going to? Some sort of Ren-Fest? Because if you are, we've got way cooler stuff you can wear."

"I don't need to be cool. Just medieval."

Seventy bucks later I left the place with some sort of gothic costume that looked like a cross between Robin Hood and Braveheart, complete with loose fitting tights and some outer tunics. The only good thing was that I could wear my Under Armour. No way was I going to freeze my butt off in Scotland.

You better appreciate this, Linna, because I have no freaking clue how I'm going to get myself into that monastery.

But that wasn't exactly true. I did have a plan. To speak French and pretend I was on some sort of pilgrimage. I mean, that's what they did back then. Only my pilgrimage would be to get Linna and get her the hell out of there before she becomes that crazy monk's next victim.

I wrote Aeden a detailed message about what I was going to do and what she needed to do just in case things didn't work out. Then, to be safe, I printed it out and sent it snail mail. No way was I going to risk having someone find something like this on my email. I could just imagine the conversation between the police and my parents. It would be ugly. And it would end with my mother crying and saying, *"We had no idea how disturbed he was."*

Yep, unless the post office really screwed up, snail mail was my best bet. I took out all the notes from Linna and gathered the stuff I needed to combine Snell's Law with the formulas for vibrations. It was Thursday night. I only had one class the next morning and a three-hour shift at the lab. That left me barely an hour to get back to 1296 before my roommates returned. *Thank you, Linna.*

Chapter Forty:
Linna

There was no way I could get to the courtyard unseen. Too many paths and too many monks returning from their afternoon tasks. But I knew another way—the forge. I could follow the beaten towpath from the garden shed to the outer wall and then walk a few yards down to the tower where the blast furnace was. From there, I could sneak around the back of the cloister wall and watch for my monk. He had to circumvent the front entrance to make his escape. That meant going directly down the hill to the cottages and the road.

I kept promising myself that once I saw him leave I'd be free to find my own way home. *You're such a liar, Linna.* The air was brisk but not frigid. Still, with a hurt ankle, it was a miserable walk. The tower was off to my left as I started for the forge. Slow and steady. No reason to hurry. Not at first, anyway. Until I had the most awful feeling that I was being watched. One of those creepy hairs-standing-on-end sensations. I stood completely still, too scared to turn around. Within seconds I knew I wasn't alone.

The scuttling sound of footsteps on the dirt path got louder and louder and I started to run, ignoring the pain in my ankle. The forge was just a few short yards ahead. I could hide in one of its alcoves and wait it out. I never looked back, pushing myself to go as fast as I possibly could. But when I reached the archway and took a step inside, someone grabbed my shoulder with one arm and covered my mouth with the other.

I could feel the heat from the furnace as I was dragged into a dark winding passageway. I tried to kick with my good ankle but it was impossible to see anything, let alone manage to hit it. By now I was flailing my arms, but the hallway was so narrow that I kept scraping them against the walls. Whoever had a grip on me was too large and too strong to fight off. So I did something that I haven't done since kindergarten. I bit the hand that was over my mouth. Mistake. Because in that instant, he pulled back long enough for me to see his face before he gave mine such a brutal smack that I fell backwards, hitting my head against the wall.

The last thing I remembered before waking up tied to a stone wall was a glimpse of fiery red hair.

Chapter Forty-one:
The Abbey, 1296

*E*ven in societies steeped in silence, secrets are hard to keep. Brother Alban knew that better than anyone. At the breakfast meal he lifted his eyes slowly and moved them about to catch every signal and gesture that the others would assume went unnoticed. It was a skill he had mastered. As a result, he was able to discern just how desperate Brother Rulf was to complete the metal smelting by dusk. That meant the wagon would be loaded by nightfall and on its way down the road, past the village, by morning.

Under ordinary circumstances it would not have been a matter for the precentor. But this time he could not let the forge workers move those wares. Did they think he was that naïve not to know what they were doing? What's more, he had taken his own risk. Had anyone seen him cutting the rope from the wagon's undercarriage, it would have meant his life. Murdered. Just like Brothers Jarvin and Trewyn.

The afternoon duties were slowly drawing to a close and Brother Alban carefully wiped the sacred ornaments before placing them back on the table near the altar. Slowly, he walked out of the church, but instead of crossing the courtyard, he took a small overgrown path that led him through the original herb garden, past the potting shed and out to the field that went directly to the forge. That's when he spied the girl.

She was only a few yards ahead of him, favoring one foot as she walked towards the forge. At first he thought of calling to her, but that would only draw attention to himself. He needed to guard his where-abouts and get his business with Brother Rulf over with as soon as possible. That's why the girl had to be told to leave. Brother Alban was truly vexed by the nonchalant way that she ambled about the premises as if it were an open field. She had become way too comfortable with the place.

He didn't mind at first, when she brought the monies from John Balliol's soldiers to him or to Brother Trewyn. A fair exchange for a sacred treasure. Even if there was nothing sacred about it. Furthermore, the monastery needed the funds, and Brother Alban, along with his two confidants, had found a way to do that.

Monies for the monastery's survival weren't the only matters that troubled Brother Alban. As of late, he harbored grave concerns about some of the monks who worked the blast furnace. They were more preoccupied with the mundane world and not the spiritual, and he feared these *conversi* may have joined for dubious reasons. However, it wasn't just their lack of devotion that alarmed him. It was something else. Something he couldn't quite explain, but he knew that they were conducting a far more sinister business than the sale of fake reliquaries. It became clear that he had to stop Brother Rulf.

Even with her slight limp, the girl was gaining ground. Brother Alban pushed himself to move faster, but his legs started to cramp. By now the girl had entered the forge and he was still yards away. He realized there was no sense in hurrying, and he slowed down long enough to allow the pain in his legs to dissipate. The girl was probably looking about the forge. He would order her to leave and then find Brother Rulf.

As he got closer to the chimney tower, Brother Alban could feel the wall of heat. With the exception of the glow coming from the fire itself, there was no other light. None of the torches had been lit. Brother Alban took a step into the dark furnace and called out. In the strange murkiness, the only sound he heard was the soft cackle from the hot embers.

He moved closer to the fire, calling out again. In the semi-darkness Brother Rulf emerged from the dark passageway and walked directly in front of Brother Alban, who wasted no time as he pointed an accusatory finger and lashed out with a stream of words. One accusation followed another. Brother Alban made it clear that all metalwork would cease immediately and no goods would leave the abbey. Only his demands came too late.

The red-haired monk shoved Brother Alban against the corner of the large chimney and delivered a punishing blow to the old monk's stomach. But Brother Alban refused to be beaten. He fought with hands that had only carried precious ornaments and vestments for worship. The men were upon each other as the rip and tear of robes became more intense. Brother Alban felt himself growing weaker but still struggled to fight. His outer robe and the vestments that adorned it had been ripped from his body, falling on the ground like a pile of rags.

By now the men were standing directly in front of the fire-pit. Even though the flames had begun to diminish, the heat was so intense that Brother Alban began to lose consciousness. In that split second, the red-haired monk threw him backwards into the flames and turned away so that he would not be forced to hear the man's terrifying screams.

Chapter Forty-two:
The Abbey, 1296

Brother Gregory felt as if someone had twisted his stomach. His hands shook and a slow nausea started to intensify. What if Brother Alban wasn't the only one thrown so brutally into the fire? He refused to let his mind think that the dark-eyed girl was killed. In all likelihood, she had run down the hill and back to her cottage. Still, Brother Gregory couldn't be certain.

He walked slowly from the large fire-pit, listening for any kind of sound, but the room was eerily quiet. He knew he would have to return quickly to the main hallway. Supper was to be served and he could not risk being absent. No one could know that he was in the forge. As a scribe, he had no business in this part of the monastery. But protocol would mean little compared to accusations of murder. The others would think he was the last to be seen with Brother Alban. Someone else would have to discover the grim deed. And he knew that wouldn't be until morning when the *conversi* who worked the furnace returned to their tasks.

As he passed the long corridor that lead to another part of the chimney tower, he thought he heard a strange noise. Some sort of scraping and pounding, flanked by a soft wailing sound. It had to be some unfortunate animal, he reasoned. Squirrels, raccoons and all sorts of creatures went to their early demise by getting trapped in tunnels and crawl spaces with no way out. But the wailing was high pitched. Not a sound he had heard before. In the semi-darkness, the small hairs on the back of his neck stood up. Brother Gregory was more than scared.

Whoever murdered Brother Alban could be setting a trap for his next victim. Without turning back, the young scribe raced out of the building and into the early evening darkness. The cold evening air was a welcome relief from the smoldering stench in the forge. He took the footpath and never looked back until he had reached the courtyard.

Below the blast furnace in a room with no light, the dark-eyed girl stopped screaming.

Chapter Forty-Three:
Ryn

I had never used artificial light with Snell's Law. This time I didn't have any choice. My roommates would be returning in an hour and Linna was stuck at the end of the 13th century with some crazed murderer. Not to mention the dilemma I faced with the matter of the vibrations. I had the formula okay, but I really hadn't quite figured out what I would set in motion to vibrate. Then, it hit me. My electric toothbrush. I set the thing next to the bathroom sink and placed a small prism directly in front of the incandescent light fixture.

Gauging the distance, I stepped in and waited. If things went well, I'd be back before the toothbrush lost its power. Yeah, I should have known better. Things never go well.

The last thing I remember seeing was my reflection in the mirror. *Is this the best you could do? You look like something out of a Monty Python movie.*

Fortunately, before I had time to think, it was over. The back of my head hit the wall and when I went to stand up, I was no longer in my bathroom.

I was standing against a stone wall in a dim candle-lit dining room. In front of me were at least forty or more monks eating around a huge horseshoe-shaped table. No one said a word. Not even when I took a step forward. I mean, vows of silence are one thing, but shouldn't they have at least noticed me? I took another step—until I was standing directly in front of an entire section. Again, nothing.

Like a delayed reaction, it registered all at once. *I'm invisible.* The vibrations were spinning so fast that no one could see me. The only thing I could think of was how fast those plastic spinning tops go before they run out of juice and fall over. I had no idea how long this would last, but I knew that when time caught up, I'd suddenly appear and scare the living daylights out of the entire abbey.

I had to make damn good use of this opportunity because it would never come again. All of the monks were in one place, and I'd eyeball each and every one of them. Linna's guy was young, that's what she said, and so I immediately eliminated most of the geriatric crowd. And the big brawny looking he-men crowd, too. They were probably the carpenters and heavy laborers. That left two or three possibilities. Still, there was someone missing. I saw an empty seat with a plate and some utensils in front of it. One of the monks didn't show up and the others kept looking at his seat as if it were cursed. Did Linna's guy succeed in knocking him off before dinner? Boy, could she pick 'em!

Meanwhile, I noticed something else. Years of careful training at middle school finally paid off. Secret sign language! These guys were talking all right, but with subtle gestures. I had mastered that art myself many an afternoon in seventh grade detention. While some signs were universal, most of these were only known to the guys sitting around the table. I figured I still had some time and I could learn fast. So I watched.

The monks who could pass as linebackers kept giving the same signs. One of the young guys, possibly Linna's monk, was talking to them. I made a mental note to keep an eye on him. The old guys gave an occasional sign, but I figured it had more to do with the lousy food in front of them than anything earth-shattering.

Quietly, I watched another one of the young monks. This one was nervous and jerky. Always a key suspect in any situation. I added him to my list as well. Without wasting any more time, I left the room, taking full advantage of my newfound invisibility. If Linna was anywhere in this monastery, I needed to find her before she decided to hook up with some medieval scribe.

Chapter Forty-four:
The Abbey, 1296

Brother Gregory awoke with a jolt. The nightmare sent beads of sweat across his brow and onto the small muslin pillow. The dark-eyed girl was trapped in some sort of dungeon, unable to escape. Her screams were unrelenting. The young monk sat up and tried to catch his breath. If he did scream out in his sleep, no one heard him. The room remained dark and quiet.

Something about the girl's shrieks in his dream set him on edge. He had heard those awful sounds before. It took him a moment to realize that they were the same shrill cries he heard coming from beneath the blast furnace. It was the girl! Not some poor unfortunate animal caught in the cellar. It was her! He got up slowly from his bed and wrapped the blanket around his shoulders. Finding his way in the dark, he exited the dormitory and started down the long corridor. A dim lantern hung from the wall, illuminating his path. It was easy for him to reach up and remove it from the small hook.

Quickly, so as not to wake any of the others, Brother Gregory made his way down the stairs and out the courtyard. The night air stung his cheeks, but he kept moving past the old Garth until he was on the path to the forge. Even with the fire extinguished, he could smell the soot and ash.

The gigantic forge loomed over the field like an ancient beast, its archway stretched open as if it were a mouth waiting to inhale its prey. Brother Gregory held the lantern directly in front of him and kept moving. He knew where he had last heard those sounds. He just had to find his way back there.

Inching his way down the steep stairwell he watched the candle inside the lantern flicker until he reached the bottom of the steps. Years of soot and smoke had blackened the stone walls of the lower part of the forge, turning the place into a dark, foreboding pit. Brother Gregory moved the lantern, looking for a passageway or opening that would take him to where he thought he had heard the sounds.

Yet there was one sound he didn't hear. The sound of the monk who crept behind him in the dark. Far enough back so that his footsteps blended with the night. Brother Gregory never heard a thing until the very instant when he felt a sharp blow to his head. In that brief snap of time, a shrill scream echoed in his ears, growing louder and louder until everything went black.

Chapter Forty-five:
Ryn, The Abbey, 1296

Okay. So much for trying to find Linna in a freaking dark monastery with next to no lighting. I mean, I admit, I didn't expect to see something out of HGTV, but for Heaven's sake, even the most medieval castles had overhead chandeliers with candles in them. This place only had wall sconces and not many of those. Talk about poverty.

I spent most of the night climbing up and down stairwells through endless corridors that connected dormitories to large sitting rooms and working areas. I even found the kitchen where I helped myself to some hard, nasty bread. Then, on to the church and a bunch of smaller rooms. But no Linna. I was getting exhausted and getting nowhere.

I remembered seeing some benches in a room that faced the courtyard and figured it would be a decent place to catch a nap. Decent. Not comfortable. My eyes had just started to close when I thought I heard something. Quickly, I jumped up and looked around. Unbelievable. One of the monks was either sleep-walking with a lantern or …. Or what? I had no idea what the guy was up to, but it couldn't be good.

With no guarantee how long I'd remain invisible, I wasn't about to take any chances and follow him. I just made a mental note of the direction he took. I could always go there in the daylight. Then, I shut my eyes again and this time they stayed shut. It was only when I felt someone shaking my shoulder that my mind suddenly registered two things—I was no longer invisible, and I'd better think of a cover story fast!

As it turned out, I had picked the most appropriate place to sleep. Apparently, this was the outer parlor where travelers and guests were expected. Even the ones who showed up direct from Boston Costume. I sat up immediately. It was dawn and a geriatric monk was speaking. I nodded and pretended to understand everything he said. So far, I got "Good Morrow" and something about "féðegest." The second part of the word sounded like guest, so I figured he thought I was a traveler. Okay by me.

The monk pointed to the building directly across from where we were standing and started to walk with me. I already knew the place. It was the kitchen. At least they were going to offer me some food. I nodded and took a few steps when a younger monk arrived and whispered something to the older one. Next thing I knew, the old guy shook his head and walked away. Seconds later, the younger one leaned over, grabbed me by the arm, and said something about "angelcyning."

"Angelcyning." It took me a second but I got it—English King. And from the expression on the monk's face, he was expecting me and needed to tell me something about the King of England. Something that was very important and very secretive. I had the same nauseating feeling I did back in my eleventh grade English class when we were reading *Canterbury Tales*. I didn't have a clue. But I was able to wing it then, and that's what I had to do now. Only this time getting the right translation meant more than a passing or failing grade, so I listened carefully.

All I could get was something about a wagon and the next morning. *Giant red flag on your paper, Ryn!* Then, just as we reached the archway to the kitchen, the monk turned and took off as if nothing happened. I was left standing in a doorway with at least five other monks staring at me. Staring and bowing their heads. They thought I was important.

Without moving a muscle, I glanced down at my ridiculous costume and that's when I knew I had seen something like it before. It was the kind of thing the king's men always wore in those dorky movies about the Middle Ages. Somehow, someone in China got it right when they sewed this thing.

One of the monks ushered me to a wooden stool and held out a bowl of something for me to eat. I nodded my head and took the dish. In the past few years I've become a little more adventurous with my palate, trying all sorts of cuisine in the Greater Boston area. But the gruel that had thickened to the sides of the wood bowl could hardly have been called cuisine.

Slowly, I placed what looked like a hand-forged metal spoon into the bowl and then into my mouth, swearing under my breath that I would never complain about Aeden's cooking again. No one seemed to notice that I was close to retching. I managed to take a final spoonful before placing the bowl next to a giant tub of water that I assumed was for washing.

I knew that if I was going to have any luck at all finding Linna, I'd have to figure out a way to ask someone if they had seen a girl with dark hair and dark eyes. But the only word for "girl" that I could remember from my brief and miserable encounter with Middle English was "maiden," and that wasn't enough. Jumbled thoughts and phrases moved around in my head until I realized that I didn't need to talk. Those monks in the dining room used sign language!

Okay, so maybe their sign language was complex, but believe me, there was a universal sign for the opposite sex. Within ten minutes I managed to ask if anyone had seen Linna. Three of the monks nodded and one of them motioned for me to step outside. I hurried as he pointed to the steep hill at the back of the monastery. Below it was a cluster of cottages. Apparently, that's where Linna went.

It was early in the day. Enough time for me to scope it out and get back if I couldn't find her. At least I had two things in my favor—the Under Armour was holding up, and apparently, no one thought I looked like the village idiot. Thank God the girl from Boston Costume didn't sell me that one!

Chapter Forty-six:
Linna

My head throbbed like the worst migraine I'd ever experienced. And I was inhaling so much dust, soot, and ash that my nostrils burned. Luckily, my eyes had gotten used to the darkness, and I could almost make out a faint light from a torch or lantern down a long hallway. All I needed to do was to find a way to loosen the rope that bound my hands to the large metal ring on the wall. But my hands were behind my back, and I didn't have a pin or nail. The only thing I did have was friction, so I just kept rubbing that rope. Unfortunately, it wasn't the rope that was getting the brunt of the movement. It was my wrists, and they were starting to bleed.

I paused to take a breath. In that moment, I could hear footsteps. Soft, steady footsteps that were headed my way. It wasn't the red-haired monk. His steps were loud and fast. This was different. This was someone else. I held still and waited. The footsteps were getting closer.

Think positive thoughts, Linna. Think positive thoughts. Someone's going to help you.

But I feared otherwise. I could see a figure coming down the staircase that led to this place. Tall. Thin. Just as he reached the bottom of the steps and started to walk towards me, someone approached from behind him. They were quick. Because all I heard was a dull thud before I realized that a man's body had fallen to the ground a few feet from me. The scream left my mouth automatically, and I don't remember when it stopped.

Chapter Forty-seven:
Ryn

Even though it wasn't raining or snowing, the slope behind the abbey was as slippery as hell. By the time I made it to the first cottage my butt was soaking wet. There was a narrow dirt road that connected it to a few other small, thatched-roofed houses. Someone was pulling a cart with firewood towards one of them. I kept my distance and watched.

The man left the cart in front of the cottage and pounded on the door. As soon as he entered, a girl came out and started to carry the firewood inside. *It couldn't be!* I started walking as fast as I could. *Linna!* She was carrying small bundles of wood and acted as if unloading it was the most natural thing in the world for her to do. I was seething and wasted no time in letting her know.

"What the heck, Linna? What did you do? Get a cottage and move in? You've gone freaking insane!"

But she didn't answer. She covered her mouth and started to run back inside. By now I was only a few feet away.

"Don't turn away from me, Linna! I mean it!"

She turned and faced me. Her eyes wide and dark. Her hair long and partially braided. And if it weren't for the fact that her face was slightly narrower than Linna's, it could have been her. I just stood there staring. My mind trying frantically to make sense of things. The girl moved her eyes up and down, studying my clothing before she spoke.

Again, something about the English King. I shrugged and waited for her to continue, hoping I'd be able to recognize at least another word or two. I didn't. She kept looking at the monastery at the top of the hill as if she was expecting something to happen. I took a deep breath and decided to try another tack.

I held out two fingers and pointed at her. Next, I pointed to my hair with a chopping motion to indicate another girl with shorter hair. Suddenly her face turned pale and she bit her lip. *She knows something. Girls always bite their lips when they know something.* I waited for a response. The girl looked as if she was about to cry and pointed to the monastery as she moved her head up and down.

It was a "no-brainer." Linna was in the monastery. Even if I couldn't find her. I was about to nod when the girl did something else. She waved her hands in the air and made a face. She made believe she was running and looking over her shoulder.

I got it! Linna was in the monastery and someone was after her. And if the girl wasn't exaggerating, it was someone big and possibly frightening.

Terrific, Linna. As if chasing after a dead monk wasn't enough, you now had to wake up the giant!

Chapter Forty-eight: Linna

I was certain he was dead. The body remained absolutely still. Whoever killed him didn't even bother to pick up the lantern that rolled a few feet away. The candle must have gone out immediately. However, the one down the passageway was still lit, and if I could only get the rope to budge the slightest bit, I could get out.

Who are you kidding, Linna. You'll die here.

My body was shaking so much that I almost didn't hear the sound. It was a soft grunt. Like the kind of moan an injured animal makes. I held as still as I could, expecting something to scurry across the floor. But nothing did. Then, I heard the sound again, and this time I knew where it was coming from—the man wasn't dead.

I desperately wanted to ask him if he was all right but all I could think of was "hath well," and I wasn't even sure if that made sense. He was still lying on the ground. I refused to take my eyes off of him. Slowly, he lifted his head and groaned with such intensity that I gasped. By now he had started to raise his body up. I could see his hand touching the back of his head. He was hit. Hit so hard that it had knocked him unconscious. Even now, he struggled to stand.

It seemed like hours but it was only a minute or so until he was able to catch his breath and take a few steps in my direction. His eyes had gotten used to the darkness and as he scanned the room, he looked directly at me. That's when I recognized him. It was my monk. My green-eyed monk who had been attacked and left for dead on the stairwell. My pulse began to quicken and it felt as if all of my senses were on overload. He kept moving towards me as if I was the reason he had come here in the first place. Did he know that the red-haired monk had taken me here? It didn't matter. All I knew was that my monk was here and we were going to get out of this cellar chamber.

I could feel his hands grazing mine as he touched the rope. It was secure. I hadn't succeeded in loosening the knot. He backed away and turned in the opposite direction. He was leaving me. My mind went wild as I desperately tried to find something I could say that he would understand. For some reason, I remembered what happened when I first arrived back in time. A man and his daughter thought I was a ghost. They yelled "Stythe" when I knocked on the door. "Stythe." It meant "Stop."

With all the force I could muster, I screamed as loud as I could.

"Stythe! Stythe!"

It was no use. The monk just kept walking. I could feel the tears welling in my eyes, and there were no words that I could have used to describe my devastation. At least Ryn wasn't here to see what a fool I had been.

Chapter Forty-nine:
The Abbey, 1296

The monks who worked the forge left the morning prayers with a heightened sense of urgency. The fire had been completely extinguished and needed to be restarted. That would take hours. Brother Rulf had already swept up the ashes and disposed of them. The larger bones were now brittle and broke easily with pressure.

While a handful of the *conversi* were privy to what had taken place, only Brother Rulf and a trusted accomplice knew that the dark-eyed girl from the village was held below in the cellar chamber. She knew too much. She would jeopardize everything. They would have to dispose of her as well. Later. When the fire was at it hottest… When his accomplice could leave the Scriptorium without being noticed. Even if it meant a day's wait.

The men moved the firewood from its stacks at the side of the chimney tower to the floor near the fire-pit. Starting with the smaller pieces, they layered it carefully so that there would be enough air to prevent it from going out. Larger chunks of wood that crackled and spit were added to the pyre. Except the fire was still too young and too cold to start smelting the metal. Like a child, it needed to grow and build its own strength. But they were hurried. The metalwork couldn't wait. They added smaller piles of wood around the circumference, hoping to push the flames forward. By mid-morning they had succeeded. The bellows once again whooshed the air forward. The ore and flux had turned to molten metal, giving off a strange glow.

Above, the chimney released a thick, grey smoke that clouded the air and spread until it hung over the cottages below. It was noon. Time for the third of the Little Hours service. Brother Rulf motioned for the others to go ahead. He would remain to make sure the fire didn't go out.

The monks exited one by one through the archway, moving in sync with the twelve chimes. Below them in the cellar, the girl with the dark eyes could feel the tears rolling down her cheeks.

Chapter Fifty:
Ryn

The girl looked at me and shrugged her shoulders as if to say, "Well, you asked where she was, now do something about it." I shrugged back and turned towards the hill. As I started to take a step, the girl said something I didn't understand and grabbed my shoulder. She pointed to her house and with the first two fingers of her hand, made the motion of someone walking downstairs as she hunched her shoulders down. She would have been great in *Celebrity Charades*. So it wasn't bad enough I had to watch out for some crazed giant guy but I had to start looking for Linna under the monastery in its creepy cellars. *Terrific.*

You'd think with all my experience in miserable underground places, I would have shrugged this one off. But something told me, that compared to what I was about to face, the catacombs in Paris would seem like an upscale villa. I took a breath, nodded at the girl and started back up the hill. I hadn't gotten very far when all of a sudden she came racing up behind me with something wrapped in cloth. I didn't reach for it right away. I'm always wary when it comes to things wrapped up in cloth. The last surprise package I took turned out to be a kitten. Aeden was ecstatic, but my parents grumbled at me for weeks.

Other surprise packages included homemade yeast and suspicious looking brownies, both from neighbors. We kept the yeast for a few weeks until it started to stink up the refrigerator, but my mother threw out the brownies immediately and threatened us with unmentionable penalties if we tried to retrieve them from the trash.

I seriously doubted the girl was about to hand over one of her pets or any mind-altering goodies, but I lifted the cloth up slowly just to be sure. It turned out to be a loaf of bread and three small candles with a primitive metal holder. *Was this what they gave their men when they went off to the crusades?* I tucked the stuff under my arm and nodded as she headed back to her cottage. It was uncanny how her every movement resembled Linna's. I looked up at the monastery and began walking.

I swore the damned slope had gotten steeper and the first building even further away. It was lousy cold outside and the fine mist kept stinging my face. *Should have brought a ski mask.* It was bad enough going downhill—but uphill? My muscles wanted to wreak vengeance on the rest of my body, and I wanted to wring Linna's neck. Instead, I kept moving. The climb was monotonous, the air was cold, and I was in a rotten mood.

Off to my left I could hear a buzzing sound. Like the kind those gnats make when you're camping. An annoying hum. Then I realized what it was. Beehives! And lots of them! They were stacked up on layers of benches. The bees just hovered around the hives, not very interested in venturing any further. I certainly had no intention of getting up close and personal either. I backed away slowly and continued up the hill. Directly in front of me was a huge chimney spewing out dark, grey smoke. *Thirteenth century air pollution at its best.* Whatever they were producing in that building, I was pretty sure Linna wasn't there. The building looked like some sort of blast furnace. The last place she'd be. I walked past it and started to take a narrow path to the center cluster of buildings, figuring she might be under the church itself or in that general area. She wasn't. Others were. Out of the corner of my eye, I saw a line-up of monks.

Line-up might not be the right word, but heck, what do you call a long single line of monks walking from the furnace building to the church? Quickly, I ducked behind some tall, bushy trees and held my breath until they passed. No sign of a giant. No sign of anything unusual. For a brief second I thought about going into the furnace and looking around since all the monks were obviously gone, but I seriously doubted that's where I'd find Linna, so I just worked my way, unseen, into the courtyard.

It was early afternoon. The bell had chimed twice. No one appeared to be in sight so I entered one of the church buildings from the large archway in front. Nothing but narrow halls and small rooms. I noticed a steep stairwell at the end of the corridor. At the base of the stairs I could see a torch hanging from the wall. Perfect for lighting my candle.

One large room led into another but no sign of Linna. No sign of anything. Just dust. I tried not to think about allergens or microbes as I made my way through the building. Finally, a few feet from me, I saw a tunnel. It was a low archway and an even lower ceiling. I was thankful for one thing—the candlelight didn't reveal all the rodent crap on the floor, but it did a fair job of pointing out lots of crawling insects. I called Linna every miserable name I could think of. It surprised me how many I knew. At least it took my mind off of the tunnel itself and that was a good thing, because the tunnel was getting tighter and the ceiling was getting lower.

At a point where I thought I might be better off turning around, I saw a dim light. The tunnel opened into another room. Probably under a different building. Unlike the other rooms, this one had wooden benches and a table. And… I could see the drippings of candle wax on top of the surface. *Someone's doing something here. But what?* It didn't appear to be the kind of place for prayer and meditation. I kept moving. My candle was almost out, and I only had two more.

It felt as if I had been walking in circles. Empty rooms, creepy tunnels, strange smells, and no sign of Linna. The last place I got to before I was able to climb back upstairs was some sort of labyrinth. Only old boxes with bones and hair tucked in the corners of the rooms. A regular treasure trove. By the time I made it back to the courtyard, it was just after dusk. Five chimes rang, and I watched from my hiding spot behind some bushes as the monks filed into the church.

The kitchen was just across the courtyard, and I snuck in, afraid to use the candle. In the dark, I managed to find some sweet stuff to drink as I washed down half a loaf of the tasteless bread. *Okay, so the girl who looks like Linna can't bake. That's someone else's problem.*

It was too dark to continue looking. I had no choice but to find a place to sleep and start over in the morning. My best bet was one of the storerooms in the kitchen. No one would be going in there tonight. I found some bundles of cloth and made myself a spot for sleeping on the floor. I must have been so tired that I fell asleep right away and never heard the monks serving dinner. I was out cold.

Under normal circumstances, like having a decent bed and mattress, I would have slept for hours. Lying face down in a pile of rags was anything but normal. No wonder the pain in my lower back jolted me awake. From that point on, it was useless. No matter what I did,

I knew I wasn't going to sleep. I stood up to stretch and in that instant, I heard the echoing of footsteps in the courtyard. And not just a few footsteps. *Did an entire army arrive?* I made my way to the door and looked out.

Then, I followed.

Chapter Fifty-one:
The Abbey, 1296

The abbot held his breath and waited. He had never done anything like this before. But one mysterious death, one murder, and one disappearance left him with three less brothers in a suspiciously short period of time. He had no choice but to call a secret meeting of his council.

Each monk was given a small candle and told to light it once the other monks in the dormitory fell asleep. Then, when the candle had reached the halfway point, they were to use it as they made their way to the abbot's house, behind the church.

One by one, the small group of men arrived and sat silently on the floor of the abbot's meeting room, waiting for the head of the abbey to speak. The silence in the room was a silence of fear, not contemplation, as the abbot took his seat in the center of the room. He nodded to each man before he spoke.

"May the Lord protect us. I have called you here because I fear there is a terrible disease spreading in our abbey. Not a disease of the flesh, but of human will. We are no longer safe to live our lives in quiet reflection and prayer. I have been informed by our herbalist that Brother Jarvin died of poisoning, not a natural death. Brother Trewyn was stabbed in our midst. And Brother Alban, our precentor, vanished without a word. I fear that he, too, has been murdered."

In the dim light, some of the monks clenched their fists while others wiped away tears. The abbot continued.

"Our monastery has flourished under the protection of King John Balliol. But King Edward I of England is now preparing to go to war against our monarch. I have it on the most trusted of sources that once he does, he will want to take over our monastery as his own property. We will be displaced—scattered about like wandering friars. I am no fool. I knew that Brothers Jarvin, Trewyn and Alban brought monies to this abbey through unrighteous and impious acts. Yet their intent was pure. Nonetheless, it cost them their lives."

The men remained silent as they moved closer to listen.

"Within this abbey are other men. Men who appear to be monks, but for them it is nothing more than a disguise and a means to commit the most heinous of deeds. Would that I knew who these men were. Alas, I do not. Be wary. I only know that they are the henchmen of Edward I. And soon, one of Edward's own men will be coming by this abbey on pretense. For certain he is here to communicate with those who plot our demise. Do not be deceived."

Suddenly, there was a gasp, as one of the men stood up and spoke.

"I fear, father, that Edward's man has already been to the abbey. Just this very morning. He appeared in the kitchen. We fed him and sent him on his way. He was seeking someone in the village. A girl."

"Beware," the abbot said as he stared straight ahead. "That man will be back. It was only a guise. And when he returns, he is to be taken to the bell tower. We cannot allow him to communicate with the traitors in our abbey. Give the word to all whom you trust. And be on guard for this man. Seize him at once."

Without speaking another word, the abbot stood up and left the room. The monks slowly rose and returned silently to their beds. Some slept while others remained awake, gripped by fear and sadness.

Chapter Fifty-two:
Linna

I tried to scream again. "Stythe! Stythe!" It was useless. The green-eyed monk kept walking. I watched as he moved down the dark corridor, never stopping to turn around. The sound of his footsteps got softer and softer. Before I could grasp what was happening, I heard a loud crashing sound. It came quickly and suddenly, followed by the pounding of metal on a wall. The forge monks must have returned to work their metal.

As fast as the sound came, it stopped and the footsteps started again. Someone was walking back towards me. I held still and counted each step until I realized who it was. My monk had returned and this time he was holding what looked like the jagged metal bottom of the lantern.

My heart started pounding so fast that I thought I would hyperventilate. Everything happened at once. My monk took the jagged metal and used it to slice through the rope. In seconds I was free. He grabbed me by the wrist and pointed to the long dim corridor, motioning for me to start running, but my legs wouldn't move.

I'd been tied to that wall for so many hours that all of my muscles were stiff. It felt as if my legs were made of lead. I was slow and clumsy as I moved closer to the few wall sconces that still emitted some candle light. The monk was barely a foot or two ahead of me and he kept motioning. Finally, in what I think must have been exasperation, he grabbed me by the waist and ushered me through the corridor. His arm held tight to my body. Instead of feeling as if I was being held hostage, I felt safe, protected and secure.

My ankle still hurt and I found myself leaning on him. The urge to get even closer was overwhelming as we made our way down the corridor. I could see a circular stairwell that rose up to the forge. It must have been part of the chimney. Formidable and solid. It also went below us, and that's where my monk took us. In slow, quiet steps we moved so far underneath the building that even the smell of soot and ash became distant. For a brief second, I swore I could hear footsteps and voices, but we kept moving. Only one lantern illuminated the long, winding passageway, and I had no idea how long that candle would last.

Please let us get out of here. I can't bear it.

Just as I thought we'd never escape from this unending labyrinth, there was another stairwell. This time we would have to climb. Only the distance between the steps was so high that it taxed every move we made. And the worst part was that there was no light. I just held on to the monk's hand as we continued our climb. I thought about counting the steps, but I knew it would only torture me. Instead, I gripped his hand tighter.

Each step seemed to take pleasure in draining me of energy. I kept moving until finally there were no more steps. Just darkness. I pressed the monk's hand even tighter, and he gave mine a quick squeeze back. I didn't know if my heart was beating from sheer exhaustion or something else.

My feet moved automatically in the darkness until I tripped on a short step, stumbling forward, and right into him. He steadied my shoulders and held me still for a moment. Long enough for my hands to start shaking. I looked up, unable to see his face clearly in the dark, but I did see something else. Moonlight. We had made it outside.

The monk must have heard the sounds before I did because he moved me closer to him and gently put his hand over my mouth. And that's when I heard the sounds as well. They were footsteps. At least five or six men making their way across the courtyard.

We held as still as possible. So close that I could feel the air going in and out of his lungs. I reached for his hand but this time, instead of holding it, he had clasped my fingers in his.

Chapter Fifty-three:
The Dark-Eyed Girl

*T*he girl closed the door to her cottage and bolted it. Then, turning to her father, she spoke.

"King Edward has wasted no time in sending one of his men to the monastery. And one who only speaks his own tongue."

The tired, gaunt man moved closer to the small fire that he had just started by the kitchen.

"I fear it is no longer safe for you to do the Brothers' bidding."

"Yey, I know. The King is clever. Sending a girl first. And she took the reliquary that we were to sell, only to return it to me when a dreadful man gave chase to us on the hill. A monk. But not like those we favor."

"All is not well on the hill, my child. The relics they fashioned gave them the bread they needed, but King Edward will take all of that away."

The girl looked down as her father continued to speak.

"What business did you have with the King's man?"

"Nay, father. He seeks the girl. And I have delayed his search. In earnest, I do not know where she may be, but I sent him beneath the abbey. King Edward will want that man's report. It will come too late."

"Say not a word more. And do not go back to the monastery."

"Yey. I understand, father. But I am troubled. For the girl that he sent appears in face and kind like me."

The man froze for an instant, waiting for the words to come.

"Then she will be in grave danger if indeed she has returned to the abbey."

"I should not have beguiled the King's man, for it may be too late for the girl."

"Hear me again, child. Stay away. The monastery is likened to a beehive. And something has caused them to stir."

The girl nodded as she added a few chunks of wood to the fire.

"The chimney fire burns hot both day and night, father. When the wind blows south I can smell the smoke."

"I fear they are no longer forging instruments and vessels for the hearth. Too many wagons move toward Edinburgh and Dunbar."

"What are you saying, father?"

"Edward I prepares for war, and the abbey may become his stronghold. The good men of the cloth will leave. Stay away. The new bees in that hive bear a lethal sting."

The girl didn't say a word as she looked out the small window that faced the abbey. In the distance, greyish smoke was still rising.

Chapter Fifty-four:
The Abbey, 1296

The hand gesture was quick. And only Brother Rulf noticed the scribe's message as they sat for the supper meal. He remained motionless as he contemplated what he had been told. Someone had written a warning to the scribe. Or perhaps a threat. Either way, the men had to dispose of the girl. They had waited too long. It would have to be done at night. Even if it meant rekindling a colder fire and hastening to clean up the remains.

The red-haired monk slid his index finger across the wooden bowl and tipped his hand slightly. The scribe nodded inconspicuously. It was agreed. The scribe had already secured the potion that would render the girl unconscious. All he would need to do was to slip down the stairs beneath the forge and cover her mouth with the tainted cloth. Then, Brother Rulf could easily dispose of the body.

Yet all had not gone as planned. The scribe had just started to descend the steep stairs into the cellar when he heard footsteps above him. He could not risk anyone finding the girl. Quickly, he backed himself into a small closet that ran the length of the stairs. It was used to store pokers, bellows, shovels and brooms. Grabbing a heavy iron poker, he waited in the dark until the other monk passed by, unaware that he was inches away from the scribe. The girl was down below. Still tied to the stone wall with a heavy metal ring. And she hadn't ceased her wailing, whimpering and shrieking. A cacophony of sounds that grated on his every nerve.

The scribe tiptoed down the stairs, lingering just a few steps from the monk, until they had almost reached the bottom. Then, with a single well-aimed move, he held tight to the poker and forced it down hard over the man's head. The monk crumbled beneath his own weight and fell forward. A few feet away, the girl continued to scream.

The scribe started to reach for the poisoned cloth that he had tucked under the rope on his waist, but it was gone. It must have slipped out when he used the poker. And now, in the semi-darkness, it would be impossible to find. The scribe had no recourse but to climb back up the stairs and steal another potion from the herbalist's pharmacy.

He reasoned that there would still be time before dawn. Time enough for Brother Rulf to dispose of the girl and the monk at the base of the stairs.

Chapter Fifty-five:
Charlotte Campbell

*C*harlotte Campbell could not put the manuscript down. It was like reaching into a bowl of peanuts, one mouthful leading to the next. In lieu of ingesting a salty treat, she was mired under layers of deceit and intrigue, finding it so fascinating that she cancelled her Friday night date and postponed a much needed grooming for her dog until the following week. With enough yogurt and salads in her fridge, Charlotte intended to keep translating throughout the weekend.

By Sunday afternoon she was exhilarated and exhausted. It was unbelievable. She discovered something that had been overlooked in Linna's original translation and in her own early deciphering. *The murderer was not acting alone.*

None of this had anything to do with Linna's disappearance in Georgetown, but Charlotte still felt compelled to give Ryn an update.

"That monastery was more fractious and dangerous than anyone could imagine. Had your girlfriend lived in that time, her life surely would have been cut short had

she discovered what was going on. I'll talk with you this week."

The email was sent on Sunday night and Charlotte figured that Ryn would get back to her at the beginning of the week. She was wrong.

Chapter Fifty-six:
Ryn

It wasn't an army. I held my breath as six or seven monks walked across the courtyard and behind the church. They weren't going to any prayer service. Not in the middle of the night anyway. When they were at least a few yards ahead of me, I made my move. Spiderman would have been proud. I crept, lurked and snuck quietly behind them and watched as they went into a small house. I didn't even know there was anything back there, and I'd spent the whole darn day looking. I don't know how I could have missed it, and then I remembered the hill. The house was built on the lower slope. No wonder I didn't spot it when I was looking for Linna.

Other than the forge, it was the one place I hadn't looked. It occurred to me they could very well have Linna tied up in there. Still, I couldn't go barreling in like some half-crazed lunatic. I had to settle for ducking low to the ground and trying to peek in the windows.

The house, if you could call it a house, was small. Each of the three windows gave me the same view—a circle of monks in dim candlelight. If Linna was there, I honestly didn't know where they would have hidden her. That left the forge. Too bad I didn't start there in the first place.

With the secret circle of monks still inside the little house, I figured it was the perfect time to head over to the forge without getting caught. At least it should have been the perfect time. Technically, there was enough moonlight for me and I had a fairly straight, even path. If I learned one thing, it was to never think things are going to be simple. No sooner did I start walking when I swore I heard Linna scream. It was only one scream, and yeah, maybe it was a screech owl or something, but honestly, it sounded like Linna. There was some sort of commotion. A fight maybe? I just kept running towards the spot where I heard that shriek. Apparently, I wasn't the only one.

The fun-filled candlelight meeting had just ended, and next thing I knew I was swarmed by a bunch of frantic monks who grabbed a hold of me and started to drag me off towards the church tower. Whoever came up with the misnomer of pious monks hadn't met these guys. There was no way I could have fought back. Not with six or seven of them. But I gave it a try.

I elbowed, I kicked, and I even managed to throw a few punches. But these guys could wield their fists as well. The worst part of it was getting knocked around a narrow spiral staircase that led to the top of the bell tower above the church. I watched the lantern in front of me wave and flicker as I got batted about. *That'll teach you, Ryn, for not letting go of an ex-girlfriend.* Finally, I gave up. I figured I might need some strength if they decided to hurl me from the belfry like something out of a bad horror movie.

One well-aimed heave and it would have been all over for me. Thankfully, it never happened. I guess either they didn't want to deal with the mess or they thought they might need me later on, because all they did was lock me in there. In retrospect, they couldn't have tied me up if they wanted to. They didn't have any rope, unless of course they were willing to part with their waistbands, and apparently, they weren't. So I was just shoved through a wooden door that bolted from the outside and left to sit in the dark under a giant bell. The wind blew in from all sides of the tower and I ducked down. Even the heavy rope that they used for the chimes was swinging. And in that instant, I realized something. Someone would be back at dawn to clang the bell for early morning prayers. And they wouldn't be alone. I had to get my butt out of there.

Chapter Fifty-seven:
The Abbey, 1296

*T*he scribe hurried back to the cellar beneath the forge. His hands were still cold from the damp night air, even though he kept them tight at his sides. He knew the herbalist's shed quite well, having watched the elderly monk prepare special inks and dyes needed for the Scriptorium. In the pitch dark, he found his way to the small vial of dwale and dosed a new linen cloth with it. This time he would be quick. Just a wave under that girl's nose and it would render her unconscious.

She had to be disposed of, yes. Still and all… she needn't suffer. She'd never wake from the potion and her body would be consumed in the fire before the other monks returned to continue smelting the metal. Brother Rulf was to arrive before dawn. Together, they'd add one more body to the pyre. The dead monk at the base of the stairs. The scribe was certain that the blow to the man's head killed him instantly.

Holding the lantern a few feet ahead of him, the scribe started down the steep stairs to the room below the fire. The girl was no longer screaming. Perhaps she had given up or destroyed her voice. Either way, he was grateful for the silence as he continued down the steps. Yet as he got closer to the base of the stairs he knew something was wrong.

The body of the monk he had killed was gone. Frantically, the scribe lifted the lantern and moved it from side to side, illuminating each of the walls in the room. Then, he froze. Directly across from him he saw the large metal ring. A few strands of rope were lying beneath it and the girl was nowhere in sight. Had Brother Rulf gotten rid of them already? It couldn't be. The fire was not hot enough and there was no lingering odor of burnt flesh. A horrific thought came to the scribe. What if the man wasn't dead after all? What if it was just a painful blow to the head? If that monk was indeed alive, then he had somehow managed to free the girl.

Without wasting a second, the scribe took to the stairs and out to the courtyard path. If the monk and that girl were freed, they could not have gone too far. He paused as he glanced in the direction of the church, straining to listen for anything out of the usual night noises. And then, he heard it—a soft, steady crunching sound that could only be made by feet stepping over the small twigs and branches that were scattered on the walkway.

He moved carefully, following the steps until he saw for himself what his mind had refused to believe. The monk and the girl were alive! They were headed for the path behind the cloisters. The path that would take them to her cottage below.

The scribe took a deep breath, blew out the candle in his lantern and charged at the pair with all the strength and fury he could muster. It happened so quickly that the last thing the girl remembered before falling to the ground under the weight of a lantern hitting her head was the one scream she was able to make.

Chapter Fifty-eight:
The Dark-Eyed Girl

The dark-eyed girl reached for another blanket at the foot of her cot. The wind had suddenly picked up, and she could feel a cold blast of air through the window near her bed. As she sank back under the covers she heard something else. A bell. The sound of the monastery bell being rung.

She stood up and walked into the foyer. Her father was still fast asleep. The wind hadn't disturbed his dreams. The girl heard the bell again. It sounded almost frantic. As if the chime itself was screaming. Her thoughts turned to the other girl. The one who looked like her. The one she had called a thief. What if that girl was being held hostage? Maybe that girl had nothing to do with King Edward after all.

The dark-eyed girl tried to dismiss those thoughts and return to sleep but the bell rang out once more. *Such an odd hour for a chime.* She crept quietly from her bed, put on the warmest clothing she could find and used the remaining embers in the fire to light the lantern she would take with her up the hill.

Chapter Fifty-nine:
The Abbey, 1296

The red-haired monk had been absent from prayer service too many times. Another absence could be considered suspect. He signaled again to the scribe seated across from him at the supper table. Two, then three, then four tapping fingers at the edge of the bowl. The scribe nodded slightly, pretending to be at prayer.

It was understood. Brother Rulf would attend Vesper services then retire to his bed in the dormitory. He would arise before dawn, kindle and stoke the furnace fire and then return to his bed and wait for the morning chime. By the time the monks had returned from morning prayers, the girl's body would be nothing but ash and dust.

While the others slept in the long, narrow room, Brother Rulf dozed on and off. Fragments of dreams lingered for an instant then vanished like smoke. And no matter how he positioned himself, his body could not get comfortable. Each movement, each turn and each stretch seemed to torment him even more. Then, just as he turned on his side, he heard the chime. He was certain of it.

Sitting upright in his bed, he listened again. A second ring. This one louder, almost desperate. And then, a third and final chime. The sounds seemed to blend with the night wind, but Brother Rulf feared they were a warning.

Quietly, he slipped into his robe and footwear, and then crept slowly down the stairs, making his way to the forge. The scribe would have taken care of the girl by now, but Brother Rulf dared not risk the fire burning out before daybreak. The goods had to be finished. Finished and loaded onto the wagon. And this time he would be watching it until he was certain it reached the road for Edinburgh and Dunbar.

Chapter Sixty:
Ryn

The rope looked long enough for me to grab onto it, swing outward from the window and rappel down the tower. There was just one problem—hoisting, climbing, swinging and rappelling weren't skills I had mastered. What the hell! They weren't even skills I was remotely familiar with. But the prospect of being hurled from a tower by a mob of angry monks gave me the impetus I needed to grab the thing.

The minute I had the rope securely in my hand and moved toward one of the windows, the bell rang out. Not a loud chime but enough to scare the crap out of me. I had to be more careful. I had to figure out how to maneuver the rope around it. The window ledge was fairly easy for me to get to, so I held out the rope and climbed up. But the wind and the dampness from the light rain made the damn thing so slippery that I accidently leaned forward, shoving the bell with so much force that it chimed again. This time much louder.

I just hoped those monks were heavy sleepers. By now I was standing straight up in the window opening, my back facing the outside. At least I didn't have to look down. Even in the dark it would have scared the crap out of me. *Thank you, Linna. Thank you, Linna. I will never, ever, under any circumstance fall for a girl again.*

In all the movies and TV shows I'd seen where the guy rappels down a mountain or down the side of a building, they always hang on to the rope and give a little jump. My feet weren't willing to do that. They were frozen on the window ledge. And that wasn't all. The wind kicking up at my back was getting old really fast. I knew if I didn't do something, I wouldn't need to rappel down. Someone would take care of that for me.

So I took a deep breath, closed my eyes, gave a tug and took the first jump. The tug set the bell ringing again but not as loud as the last time. Then, I leaned back for more balance and momentum, each time kicking the tower harder with my feet. I was starting to get the rhythm of it. Until I couldn't kick any more. The rope only went part way down.

I swore it was a longer rope. It looked as if it went for yards all coiled up around the metal wheel that went around the bell. Maybe it got stuck on something. Or maybe it wasn't that long after all. What the heck did it matter? It wasn't as if I was about to file a complaint with the manufacturer. Even at the halfway point, I was about to fall to my death at the bottom of tower.

The wind decided to pick up a bit more as if I didn't have enough issues. I turned my head and looked around me. Just the monastery and the hill. But then, in the distance I saw something. A dim, flickering light from below the hill. My eyes were glued to it as it bounced and wavered in the dark. Someone was coming my way.

Chapter Sixty-one:
The Abbey, 1296

The man charged with all of his weight at Brother Gregory's back. Just as the young monk started to fall forward, the man swung his lantern with full force at the girl's head, but not before she was able to let out a piercing scream. For a brief second, both Brother Gregory and the girl were lying face down on the ground, their bodies crisscrossed on the path between the courtyard and the forge. Not for long. That changed the moment the young monk caught his breath and quickly rose. Without wasting a second, he spun around and lashed out at his attacker with an elbow to the man's waist. In the melee, Brother Gregory had no idea that the person he was fighting was also a scribe like him.

The man dropped the lantern and delivered a sharp blow to Brother Gregory's jaw. The result was instantaneous. Brother Gregory stepped back so as not to catch the full brunt of the blow and returned the punch with equal force. It didn't matter. The attacker was not willing to engage in a fair fight. He reached down, grabbed the lantern from the ground and wielded

it at the monk's chest. It was so sudden and so strong
that it momentarily took Brother Gregory's breath
away. And in that instant, the man bent down, lifted the
girl and carried her quickly towards the forge. He never
heard the footsteps of the monks who returned to their
dormitory from the abbot's house. And they never
knew that Brother Gregory was lying unconscious just a
few feet from their path.

The acrid smell in the air grew stronger as the scribe
got closer to the building. He reasoned that it must be
nearing dawn and the fire was getting rekindled.
Sufficient for the deed he had to do. As he continued to
walk, the weight of the girl got heavier with each of his
steps, forcing him to stop for a moment.

He set her down against a low stone wall and drew
a few short breaths. However, something didn't feel
right. It was as if someone was watching him and
waiting for an opportune moment to strike. The scribe
took a step back and looked around. He could discern
only the shadows of the buildings. A growing fear
began to fester in his mind. Had Brother Gregory
recovered from that blow to his chest? Impossible!
Then what?

The scribe moved closer to the stone wall where he
had left the girl. And then, out of nowhere, a well-
aimed rock landed directly over his eye, and he
stumbled backwards. His feet scuffled as he raced to
stand up, but the force of the rock had gashed the skin
above his eye and a fast flow of blood flooded his

cheek. Frantically, he started wiping his face, all the while approaching the low wall. But the girl was gone.

He couldn't fathom what was happening. A few feet from him, the girl was running back towards the courtyard and she was screaming. Only this time, it was a scream for help and a scream so loud that even the wind couldn't silence it.

Chapter Sixty-two:
The Dark-Eyed Girl

*I*t was bloodcurdling. A chilling sound. The dark-eyed girl shivered the moment she heard it. It was a cry for help, and it was a girl's voice. It had to be the one who looked like her, she reasoned. Worse yet, it sounded as if that girl was about to be killed.

The dark-eyed girl was only a few yards from the cloister building. If she hurried, she could run between the bell tower and the front of the church to follow that sound. Without wasting a second, she took off running, her lantern swaying recklessly in front of her.

The slope was steepest as she reached the top, and no matter how hard she pushed herself, her body could only move one step at a time. Her breath became fast and ragged as she got closer to the tower. Even though she was familiar with the knoll, it was as if the tower kept moving further away. The dark-eyed girl refused to slow down.

To her relief, everything changed once she made it over the berm. Taking a deep breath, she sped past the tower to the front of the church and headed straight for the courtyard.

The wind and rain were at her back but she swore she heard another sound. Like a faint "psst… psst" coming from overhead. "Rustling of bats," she thought. "It must be getting close to daybreak for them to return to the belfry."

Rushing, she charged down the path to the courtyard, but in the semi-darkness, all she could see was a stone wall.

Chapter Sixty-Three:
Ryn

I watched that damn light bounce until I thought I'd go out of my mind. It was getting tougher and tougher to hang onto the rope, but I kept telling myself that whoever was coming up the hill would be able to help me. It was unnerving. I swore I heard Linna scream. Loud and clear. "Help!" I was going mad. Dangling off a tower from a rope that was too short to reach the ground will do that to you. Still, I was sure it was her, and I had to get off this tower. I just kept telling myself that the person with the lantern would help me. Yeah, I was nuts. Inventing delirious lies.

At least those lies kept me sane for a few minutes. Then, like Linna dropping me after high school and telling me to "move on," the person waving the lantern light skirted the blasted tower and headed for the courtyard. It was only when I worked up the courage to swing my body around, I saw who it was.

The girl. That blasted dark-eyed girl from the cottage who sent me on the wild goose chase through the monastery underground. I tried to get her attention. Anyone in their right mind would know that "Psst!

Psst!" meant "Hey, you. Look over here!" Even if it wasn't exactly Old English. It was a sound, for Heavens' sake, and she should have recognized it!

But no… she just kept moving. By now, I was losing my grip on the rope, and it felt as if my body was getting heavier as I swayed like a pendulum back and forth from the wall. Occasionally, one of my feet would get stuck in a small crevice between the stones. Just like the Bastille. And suddenly, something occurred to me. I had *scaled* that Bastille inner tower. And I did it by using the tips of my fingers. This couldn't be much different. Just colder. And windier. And darker. Still, it was my only way out.

All I needed to do was reach for the first decent crack with one of my hands and then let go of the rope with that hand. Next, find a good indentation or ledge, jam a foot into it and pray to the gods that I could hang on.

I let the momentum from the wind move me closer to the tower. It paid off. I found the same foothold that I discovered randomly by moving my leg around. I was halfway there. At least for the first step. Taking a breath, I let go of the rope with my right hand and moved it across the stones. I felt a small groove right away. Carefully, I moved my left foot down a few inches until it, too, met up with a crevice. I was on my way. All I had to do was let go of the rope with my left hand and reach quickly in search of another crack.

I know it happened in an instant. A blink. But it seemed as if the time-space continuum stretched out every second and nanosecond. I had thoughts of dying a slow and agonizing death. *Who was I kidding?* Reality returned and I knew it would be a swift and immediate demise. I let go of the rope and slammed my left hand into the wall as my fingers searched for another hole. *There's got to be a hole. There's got to be a hole. The mason work wasn't that precise.*

After what seemed like hours, my fingertips found a secure hollow and I was able to breathe again. I had started my descent. No rope. No turning back. I remembered the way we did it in the Bastille. Not straight down. Never straight down. I knew enough to stick my leg out and take a lower sideways step.

I wondered how many turns it would take around the tower for me to get down. Five? Seven? Ten? I told myself ten, because if I thought it was going to be five or six, and I passed five or six turns, I'd go insane. This way, I settled on ten. And if I got down sooner, then hallelujah for me.

Chapter Sixty-four:
The Abbey, 1296

The fire was still burning in the pit of the forge when Brother Rulf entered. It was a clean fire—just wood. No lingering stench of burnt hair or flesh. No sign of death. That unnerved the red-haired monk. The scribe was supposed to rid them of the girl. It should have been so easy for him. She couldn't weigh much, yet the fire would still be consuming her body. Unless the scribe found another way.

Brother Rulf paced in front of the fire as he added more wood. Perhaps the scribe could offer a sign at the Lauds prayers. Then the red-haired monk would know for certain what had become of the girl. But one thing was clear—he alone would have to dispose of the other body. He could no longer trust the scribe.

It would be dawn soon and the fire had to be at its hottest. The wagon was already set and ready for loading. The horse would be delivered from the grange. King Edward's men were waiting on the road to Edinburgh. Another contingency was waiting as well, further down towards Dunbar. It was paramount that the goods be delivered as planned. Brother Rulf knew that time was running short. Time they desperately needed for more metal to be smelted and formed.

All he had to do was to dispose of the body at the foot of the stairs. The body that belonged to another scribe. Brother Gregory. And why that unlikely scribe had ventured into the forge at all was a mystery for the red-haired monk. Shaking his head, Brother Rulf stepped away from the fire and walked toward the stairwell that led to the cellar room.

Hurriedly, the red-haired monk went down the steps. He would have to act quickly. Grab the body. Carry it upstairs. Toss it into the hot flames. For a flicker of a second he thought of Brother Alban and the burning coppery smell that lingered in the air. Its acrid odor permeated his nostrils. This would be no different.

A faint lantern light illuminated the stairwell as Brother Rulf got closer to the bottom steps. He looked down, expecting to see the body of Brother Gregory, but all he found was an empty room.

Had the scribe deceived him? Did he sneak in here instead to free the girl? And what about Brother Gregory? Maybe he wasn't dead after all.

The red-haired monk thundered up the steps and back to the fire pit, his face as crimson as the flames in front of him. His pulse quickened and his heart began to pound. He needed to find the scribe, but all he could do was to stoke the fire.

Chapter Sixty-five:
Linna

Even with the sharp pain that ran from the top of my head to the roof of my mouth, I was able to reach down, grab a rock from the ground and throw it as hard as I could at my attacker. He thought I was still unconscious but he thought wrong. I had waited until just the right second before I took aim. I knew I couldn't afford to miss my mark.

I didn't expect him to fall backwards, but as soon as I saw him stumble, I took off running. The moon and starlight were starting to fade as the sky began to lighten. It was approaching dawn. Only a few seconds before the man would reach me. I'd be the only figure running on the dark path, an easy target. Thankfully, the stone wall was low and concealed by dense bushes in some spots. All I had to do was get to one of them and hide.

My head throbbed and every movement seemed to radiate pain. I half expected my monk to find his way in the dark and reach me, but I knew that he, too, had been injured. How badly, I had no idea. It was a nightmare. I had to keep moving even though the wind pressed into me like a vise, trying to slow me down. I screamed at the top of my lungs hoping that someone would hear me. But all I was doing was letting my attacker know where I was. I forced myself to stop, clamping my lips together until they were numb.

In the faint greyish light, I saw a small opening between two heavy clumps of brush and trees. Without wasting a second I ran as fast as I could and scrambled over the wall until I was safely on the other side. Bending down low to the ground, I crept alongside the wall until I reached the place where the trees and brush were so thick that no one could find me. Exhausted, I knelt down and waited.

My monk had to return. I'd hear him. Even if the wind tried to silence his footsteps.

Chapter Sixty-six:
The Dark-Eyed Girl

A gust of wind and the candle flickering in the dark-eyed girl's lantern was snuffed out. The screams had stopped as well. Blinded by the darkness, she stood still and waited for her eyes to adjust, hoping she would hear one more sound that would take her to the other girl. But instead, all she heard was the wind as it rustled the tree branches.

That same "psst, psst" noise seem to permeate the air as the dark-eyed girl continued to walk down the path from the courtyard to the forge. Without warning, she tripped over a large branch that was blocking the walkway. Her lantern rolled off to the side, out of her reach. As she started to stand up, she had a strange, sickening feeling that she wasn't alone.

She realized too late that it wasn't a branch. It was the leg of a man who deliberately forced her to fall. As she turned to run, he grabbed her with both arms and started to pull her in the direction of the forge. The dark-eyed girl allowed herself to go limp for just a moment. Enough to catch the man off guard. Without hesitating, she swung at him, unleashing a strength and anger she didn't know she possessed.

Her fists found their way into his throat, forcing him to cough, but she was no match for his size and muscle. He delivered a fast kick to her thigh followed by another to her shin. This time it was her scream that split the night air in half.

Chapter Sixty-seven:
Ryn

〜

Unbelievable. How that dark-eyed girl could walk by and not hear the noises I was making was beyond unbelievable. Unless she was ignoring me on purpose. I tried again. "PSST!" Nothing. She just kept walking as if she was Little Red Riding Hood on her way to deliver a basket. *Well I've got news for you, kiddo, grandma's not waiting at the other end!*

It was useless. I had already started free climbing my way down the tower, poking around for ridges, cracks and any tiny openings that would enable me to hold on. By my count, I had made two complete turns around the tower. The death plummet was still there. Eight more turns to go. I twisted my head around to see if I could get a glimpse of the girl but she was already by the courtyard. *What is it with these girls?*

I started to move my left leg down a few inches to reach for another notch when a scream from hell took me by surprise, and I let go with my right hand. I was wobbling. Wobbling with less than a second to find another opening for my foot. *Can't believe I'm freaking dangling from a tower because of a girl.*

The scream stopped. At least I thought it stopped. My mind just switched into a zone I never knew I had. I was suddenly focused. My foot felt a small crevice and I latched on. From that point I just moved automatically. Like a zombie, incapable of any other thoughts. One foot, then a hand, then the other foot, the other hand. I kept going. Was it five turns? Six? It didn't matter. I told myself it was five and I kept climbing down.

Just when I thought I actually had a good chance of making it to the bottom, the wind started to pick up and rain began to pelt the entire tower making it as slippery as hell. There was no way I was going to keep my grip.

Chapter Sixty-eight:
Brother Gregory

*T*he sudden and unexpected blow to his chest, coupled with the pain in his body from being hit and hurled down the cellar steps was overwhelming for Brother Gregory. His physical agony was nothing compared to the anguish he felt when he realized that the dark-eyed girl had been abducted once again. Worst of all, he knew the attacker. When you sit silently next to someone for days on end, weeks at a time, and month after month, you recognize their very being.

Brother Gregory knew that the dark-eyed girl was about to be killed by the scribe with whom he had shared his parchment and his ink. As he stood up he could see that the sky was changing color. The blackness had turned to heavy grey. And in that moment, he began to feel the force of heavy droplets of rain. Unlike other storms that began with a soft drizzle, this one sent shards of glasslike pellets into his skin.

Quickly, Brother Gregory raced to the forge. Even in the rain he could smell the acrid smoke coming from the chimney. If he had any chance at all of saving the dark-eyed girl, he couldn't afford to waste a second.

As he ran through the rain all he could think of was how his pulse quickened when he clasped his fingers in hers. Linked. Entwined. He wasn't letting go of all he believed in, but he was admitting that the spiritual world was no longer enough.

The smoke got thicker as he approached the forge and he prayed he wasn't too late.

Chapter Sixty-nine:
The Abbey, 1296

The monk assigned to ringing the bell shuddered when he stepped out in the morning rain. It was just dawn and the murky sky refused to lighten. The man walked slowly to the tower, prepared for his daily climb to toll the Lauds bell. Time to call the others to prayer.

From the tower, he would go to the church to light the candles. For a brief instant, the acrid smell of smoke brushed his nostrils, but he didn't give it much thought. Residue perhaps from the forge. He walked quickly to the tower to escape the rain. No sooner had he reached the open archway when his eye caught the figure of a man running from behind the tower to the courtyard. The man was yelling at the top of his lungs. Something incomprehensible, but frantic.

The bell ringer turned from the tower to get a better look at the man but the rain began to pick up and all he could see was a dark shadow racing toward the forge. The sky had turned a lighter shade of grey. Dawn. The monk took to the stairs and didn't turn back.

Chapter Seventy:
Ryn

Don't let anyone tell you that when you're about to die you see your whole life flash in front of your eyes. All I saw was a maze of grey and all I felt was the drenching rain as it soaked my entire body. My hands slipped. It was as simple as that. The sudden cloudburst coated the stones with a sticky rain and I couldn't hold on. And not that I didn't try. At least I thought I did. But once I lost my grip, my feet began to slip as well. I reached for another spot on the tower. Any spot. It didn't matter. My hands moved wildly in that frantic second when I knew it was too late.

It happened so fast that I couldn't even curse Linna under my breath. I had no breath. I was just falling and bracing myself for the end. What I got instead was a sudden thud to the ground. I rolled down the wet grassy knoll until I landed face down in the muck.

Aeden would have called this moment "seren-dipitous" or "fortuitous" because I happened to fall from the part of the tower that was built over the knoll. I only fell six or seven feet, not thirty. If I was still on the other side I would be dead. Splattered on the walkway. Yeah, I was lucky. That is if you consider lying soaking wet in a pile of mud and grass a stroke of luck. I'll give it that much. I was alive.

I scrambled up from the ground and moved as fast as I could to the tower. From there the courtyard would be directly ahead. And if that scream was coming from Linna, then I had to create a diversion. I'd seen enough TV and movies to know that creating a distraction always stopped the attacker or the killer. At least momentarily. But what if Linna was screaming about something else? And what if it wasn't Linna? My mind played "Twenty Questions" with me as I kept running. Finally, I realized something. The biggest question of all. What the heck was I going to do once I got to her?

Chapter Seventy-one:
The Abbey, 1296

From his vantage point in the belfry, the monk could see a man running past the courtyard towards the forge. Only that wasn't all he saw. In the open field that led to the large chimney he saw someone being dragged against their will. At times the person struggled against their combatant but they were losing ground.

The bell ringer wasted no time. He immediately started to toll the bells. Not the gentle call to Lauds prayer but a fervent clang and pitch that woke every monk in the dormitory. The bells tolled ceaselessly as the monks struggled to grasp what they were hearing. Not the death knell, not the Angelus Bell, but something so loud, so strong and so urgent that all semblance of order was momentarily lost as the men donned their robes and headed down the stairs to the courtyard.

Outside, the greyish dawn still looked like night. The rain continued to pour and the wind refused to give up.

Chapter Seventy-two:
Linna

*I*t took me a second to recognize the odd tapping sound. It was footsteps. Coming from the pathway on the other side of the stone wall. The wind and now the rain were muffling the sound. I stood up and leaned over the edge, making sure that the brush and trees kept me hidden. My monk. It *had* to be my monk.

I was jubilant. But as I started to lift one leg over the wall I could see that it wasn't my monk. It was the girl. The one from the cottages below. The one who was selling the reliquaries. I couldn't fathom why she would be here at dawn. Was someone planning on meeting her? I moved my leg back over the wall and just as it touched the ground, the girl disappeared from my sight. She had fallen and the light from her lantern went out. No matter how hard I strained to get a good look down the path, all I could see were shadows.

The next thing I knew, the girl was screaming. It was definitely a girl's scream—shrill, loud and high-pitched. It had to be hers. The worst thing about it was the fact that the scream didn't stop. Not right away. It just seemed to trill and roll on and on until it slowly faded. In that split second of time, I knew just what was going to happen—she was about to be killed.

My attacker found her. He thought she was me! I had to do something, but my feet couldn't move. I was suddenly paralyzed by fear. The wind kept whistling, the rain wouldn't stop, and worst of all, I swore I heard Ryn's voice.

I was losing my mind. And the green-eyed monk was nowhere in sight.

Chapter Seventy-three:
Ryn

"Linna! Linnnaaa!" I was screaming my lungs out as I ran down the footpath. She was out here somewhere in the rain and the darkness and I was hell bent on finding her before it was too late. I had a sneaky suspicion that the dark-eyed girl from the cottage knew exactly where Linna was. I kept yelling.

"LINNNAAA! LINNAAHHH!"

On top of it all, the bells started ringing. Not the sweet church sounds you hear in towns and university campuses but some loud crazy non-stop frantic ringing. I pictured Quasimodo hanging from the bell itself as I kept running. For just a few seconds, it started to lighten up and the rain wasn't as intense. Long enough for me to see someone else running toward the forge. A tall monk. I couldn't be sure if he was one of the men from that secret group in the little house, but it didn't matter. I just took off after him.

For a group of men who didn't get a heck of a lot of exercise, this guy was fast. At least it seemed that way. I was exhausted from my own personal physical fitness program on the top of the bell tower. No matter how hard I pushed my legs, I just couldn't reach him.

I stopped to take a deep breath and it was like someone set my lungs on fire. I was inhaling smoke and soot. I must have been so intent on chasing after that guy that I didn't notice the smell in the air. Someone was stoking a hell of a fire in that forge.

Chapter Seventy-four: Brother Gregory

he footsteps seemed to be at Brother Gregory's heels. Someone was chasing him. And even though the forge was just a few yards ahead, the young monk was terrified at the thought of who might be right behind him.

By now the smoke was getting thicker and the heat from the fire, more intense. Brother Gregory could hear the person screaming but the words made no sense—"Linnaaaa! Linnaaaa!" The monk quickly turned from the path and darted into the narrow building that linked the forge to the rest of the abbey.

Once inside, he ran down the winding passageways until he reached the opening in front of the chimney tower. There, directly in front of him he could see the scribe dragging the dark-eyed girl into the building. He started to yell but the sound of the bells clanging and echoing made it impossible to be heard.

Brother Gregory started towards them when up from behind came an outstretched arm that grasped him by the shoulder and spun him around. He was face-to-face with the red-haired monk and the last thing he remembered was the knelling of the bells.

Chapter Seventy-five:
Linna

I kept hearing my name over and over again. It was Ryn's voice. Loud and unrelenting. None of this made sense. I was losing my mind. I never should have done this. I've sent some poor girl to her death and lost my green-eyed monk for good.

The smell of smoke intensified as I climbed back over the wall and onto the path.

"Linnnaa! Linnaa!"

I heard my name again. I was sure it was my name. Even though the bells were clanging like mad and the wind was still howling, I was sure it was my name. This time I yelled back.

"Ryn! Is that you? Ryn! Over here! Ryn!"

The voice stopped and I began to think it was just my imagination. Not for long. I heard another sound. Footsteps and lots of them. Down the pathway and across the courtyard, the monks were starting to gather. I couldn't allow myself to be seen. I ducked down and waited for them to make their way to the church, but none of them moved.

Then, as if on cue for some bizarre stage play, someone came running towards me. It was still too dark to see their face but I recognized their clothing. Even drenched with rain I could see that it was regal clothing. Complete with the Royal Arms of England on it. One of King Edward's men. I started to piece together what I had seen in the wagon, and I knew what was about to happen.

The dark-eyed girl had gotten in the way. She'd be killed. The King's man was here to make sure that nothing compromised what those forge monks were supposed to deliver. I climbed back over the wall and waited. In the distance, the girl had stopped screaming and all I could hear was the wind.

Chapter Seventy-six:
The Abbey, 1296

The red-haired monk stifled a quick laugh as his fingers pressed into Brother Gregory's skin. It was ironic how the young monk who had narrowly escaped death only hours before managed to walk right back into Brother Rulf's grasp.

The red-haired monk wasted no time. He shoved Brother Gregory into the wall and watched as the man slid slowly down to the floor. All he had to do was drag the unfortunate monk to the furnace fire and wait for it to consume him. But a sudden commotion in the archway made him turn his head and that was the instant that Brother Gregory grabbed an iron poker and swung it at the red-haired monk's knees. The man buckled from the pain, and then, with a fury that matched the fire in the chimney, he went after the young monk with both fists, unable to contain his anger.

Terrified, the young monk fought back. Partly instinct. Partly determination. The furnace blazed just a few feet away as the men inched closer in their struggle.

Chapter Seventy-seven:
Ryn

If Linna was here, she was doing a damn good job of concealing it. *Fine, Linna. Live happily ever after with your precious monk. I'm done with this.* I reached down to my side and felt the small glass prism pressing into my skin. My tights might have looked medieval but they were made in China and sewn with pockets. And the one thing I took with me when I left Boston was my ticket back to the 21st century. All I needed was sunlight and I could kiss this monastery good-bye.

Sunlight. Not any time soon. The sky was grey and murky as hell, and I wondered when it would stop raining. At least the one thing that did stop was the bells. By now I was past the courtyard and getting closer to the forge. I had no idea that a few yards behind me, all of the monks in the abbey had gathered.

I tried one more time to shout out for Linna. *Your time's up, lady. It's now or never. I've got a life too, you know.* A last ditch effort. One final shout. This time I actually thought I heard her. The voice was coming from the field behind the low stone wall. I looked for a spot that wasn't covered with brambles or bushes and prepared to hoist myself over when I heard her speak.

"Ryn! Is that you? Oh my God! Ryn! You're not safe. Get out of here. I just saw one of the King's men. There must be more. They'll stop at nothing to make sure they get what they want. Get out of here!"

I wanted to yell back, "Good to see you, too, Linna." But I didn't. It was bad enough having the monks from hell drag me to the belfry. Now I have to run from the King's men, too?

I shouted back.

"Stay where you are and don't move. I'll make a run for it and hide in the forge. I'll be back as soon as I give the King's men the slip. Stay put!"

Before Linna could say a word, I ran back to the footpath and sprinted towards the large chimney tower that was spewing smoke.

Chapter Seventy-eight:
The Abbey, 1296

The bell ringer rushed to greet the throng of monks who had gathered in the courtyard. He had no idea that it wasn't the entire monastery. When the first bell tolled, the *conversi* monks instead slipped unseen to the back of the forge, taking the rear stairwell and an underground passageway.

Despite the rain, the monks in the courtyard could still smell the acrid smoke coming from the forge. Silently, they signaled one another. It was the same message. *"Something is amiss."*

In the corner nearest the cloister, a small cluster of monks edged closer to each other. They were the same monks who, only hours before, had met secretly with the abbot. Their faces filled with alarm. The two monks who had agreed to climb the bell tower before dawn were nowhere in sight. Had they taken care of the King's man before the ringer reached the belfry? The monks had no idea. Then, one of them mouthed the sentiment that all of them were thinking.

"Perchance our missing brothers have done the deed and are carrying off the body. In the dark they would not have been seen by the bell ringer."

Another replied.

"Let us pray that indeed this is so."

The bell ringer motioned for the monks to move closer. Vows of silence only permitted them to speak and conduct business in the cloister parlours and only when approved by the abbot. As the abbot was not present, the bell ringer had no choice but to speak.

"I have witnessed a frightful deed and therefore I have summoned you here. Someone is being dragged against their will to the chimney tower. We must act at once!"

Before the robed men had time to process what they were hearing, the bell ringer spoke again.

"We are not an angry mob; we are men of the cloth. I ask that only the youngest and the swiftest of our brothers run to the forge as fast as they can. The early morning service is to begin and all others shall now enter the Nave of the church."

Upon hearing his words, five or six men took off down the path and the others slowly walked into the sanctuary. Inside the nave of the church, the abbot tried to ignore the tremor in his hands as he prepared for the morning service. However, the one thing he could not ignore was the guilt that was building up inside of him.

He nodded briefly to the sacrist who was fast at work lighting candles and placing the sacred vessels.

Without Brother Alban, the sacrist had started to take over the service arrangements until the abbot could appoint a new precentor. But as of late, everyone was suspect and the abbot began to question the decisions he had made well over a year ago.

He remembered that day well. It was the day the *conversi* had first joined the abbey. Just one or two monks at first. Men who traveled from London to Sunderland and then on to Edinburgh. They knew how to smelt metal and make the utensils so needed in the abbey. Later, other brothers from England joined them. With them came a secrecy and sinister silence. By the time the abbot knew that a rift had formed between the *conversi* and the established brothers, it was too late.

The abbot had his suspicions about the forge. It needn't run for days at end, yet the smoke continued to fill the air. Did they need to trade so many wares? What about the deaths? What about Brother Alban's disappearance? Worst of all, a King's man was in their very abbey. That had to be the reason the bell ringer sent out the alarm. The abbot feared the worst. King Edward's army could not be far behind.

Chapter Seventy-nine:
The Dark Eyed-Girl

The scribe covered the dark-eyed girl's mouth with one hand and held tight to her waist with the other as he moved further into the forge. He could see the flames in the fire pit changing hues. Soon the fire would be at its hottest. He called out, expecting Brother Rulf to answer, but instead all he heard was a thrashing and pounding coming from the side alcove that led into the big room.

As he moved closer, tightening his grip on the girl, he could see the red-haired monk going blow to blow, fist to fist, with Brother Gregory. He knew it wasn't an even match. Not even close. Brother Gregory didn't stand a chance against the strength and rage of the other man. The scribe turned his attention back to the girl as he inched his way closer to the fire-pit.

Sulfurous smoke hung in the air and burnt his nostrils as he kept moving. The girl darted her eyes around, looking for any means of escape. That's when she saw the King's man. Soaking wet, out of breath and running towards her.

He was just a few feet away, screaming something unrecognizable. Something in his own tongue. As he made a move towards her, a monk who had just emerged from the passageway in the cellar below, grabbed him and twisted his arm ruthlessly. But the King's man was fast. He spun himself around and with all his force, stretched out his leg and delivered a solid kick to the monk's thigh. Reeling from the sudden pain, the monk fell back, crashing into one of the many stacks of heavy firewood.

The King's man could still see the scribe struggling to gain control over the girl. Every movement, every action, compounded the chaos in the room. The pounding and thrashing from the fight that was taking place behind him got louder as those men approached the furnace. The King's man knew they were doomed. In an instant, the flames would catch their clothing and they would both be consumed.

Even in the dim light, he saw the terror in the girl's large, dark eyes. Terror that was nothing compared to the primal fear that he felt as he watched the scene being played out in front of him.

Chapter Eighty:
Ryn

In retrospect, I would have been safer hanging out in the bell tower. Actually, I would have been safer anywhere except the damn forge! But the last thing I needed was to be chased by the King's men. Linna was insistent that she saw one of them. There's never just one of them. It's like cockroaches or ants. You only see one, but believe me, there are hundreds more.

So I raced to the forge, figuring that I could hide out in some corner or alcove, then sneak back to get Linna. Logically, it made sense. But Linna's obsession with that monk was about to cost me my life.

My feet barely touched the ground as I raced through the large archway and into the furnace room. The smoke got into my lungs immediately and my eyes began to burn. No sooner did I start to wipe them with the sleeve of my tunic when I saw that dark-eyed girl from the cottage fighting off a guy who looked like the Wolverine. I was just waiting for the blades to come out of his hands.

So I yelled. In English. "Let go of her! Let go of her!" It probably sounded like senseless babble to them.

But I kept yelling, all the while racing closer to them. I knew the guy could pulverize me with one or two blows, but what else could I do? It wasn't as if I could use the element of surprise. He had to see me heading straight for him. Yep, straight for him with no plan in mind. I figured I would just start fighting and hope for the best. At least I could see the enemy. Or so I thought.

I felt an excruciating pain as someone came up from behind me and twisted my arm until I thought my bones were going to crack. I didn't have time to think. Maybe that was a good thing because I leaned forward, spun around and kicked that guy so hard in his thigh that he fell over into a pile of firewood. The crash was loud enough to rattle the chunks of wood, but that wasn't the only noise. A hell of a fight was going on behind me and I froze.

It wasn't the fight that set every nerve in my body into overdrive. It was the location. In a matter of seconds, the two men were about to catch on fire. They were inches from the furnace and the flames were shooting orange and blue sparks.

Chapter Eighty-one:
The Abbey, 1296

The red-haired monk had Brother Gregory's head pinned to the ground. Sparks from the furnace grazed both of them as they continued to struggle. Brother Rulf hadn't planned on killing this man. It wasn't like murdering the others—Jarvin, Trewyn and Alban. Those men were deliberately sabotaging the red-haired monk's plans to turn the abbey over to King Edward I. Making those fake reliquaries and selling them to keep King John's money coming. It was futile. Scotland would have a new king. An English king. And the monastery would be his place of residence while he gathered his troops for war.

Brother Rulf pressed his weight against the younger man's body and held him to the ground. The heat from the furnace was becoming intolerable. As he struggled to hold the man back, the red-haired monk remembered the day that he and his little brother set off for the abbey.

"You'll be no more taken for a monk than that deer grazing in the distance."

"Aye, but you shall. With your years of Latin and Greek study under father's tutelage, you were always the scholar I could never be. Together, we must work this ruse for our King."

"You know how to forge iron, Rulf. You've worked for the castles in Essex. Say very little and work very hard."

"And you as well, little brother. We will find our way in the separate parts of the abbey. Others will join us. We'll know who they are. Within a year's time we shall have a plan in place for King Edward."

"And those who try to thwart us?"

"They must meet their end."

"King Edward will want an accounting."

"Then he shall have one. No doubt you will gain favor in the Scriptorium. Hide the deeds in your translations. You are clever, my brother. And no one will suspect a thing."

In that instant, a spark grazed the red-haired monk's eyelash and he winced in pain. A few feet away his brother struggled to bring the dark-eyed girl closer to the fire. Neither of them noticed the man who just entered the room.

Chapter Eighty-two: Linna

Ryn. I couldn't believe it. Ryn! I couldn't be hallucinating. It was too real. I knew that voice. As much as I hated to admit it, I was glad to hear that familiar yell. It had to be him. But it was impossible to tell where he was standing, and when I tried to look, all I could see were the monks gathering in the courtyard and one of the King's men heading right towards me. I had to stay hidden. I was making things worse. In trying to warn Ryn, I sent him right towards the forge. Right into a trap that the King's men and those monks were setting. And I'd done the same thing with *my* monk the night he followed me into the labyrinth below the wine cellar.

The cascade of events was confounding ever since I arrived. It was as if I had set everything in motion myself by interfering with time. Ryn warned me, all right, but I was too headstrong to believe him. Something intangible and incomprehensible made me resist all logic. I didn't want that monk to be murdered, but that wasn't the only reason I borrowed time. When I first started translating the words he had written, I felt as if I was meant to be with him. And then I knew for certain I was right the minute the green-eyed monk clasped his hands in mine. *Destiny. My Destiny.* I had to come back to this time and place. It was as if the parchment found me in Georgetown.

But why did Ryn come here? He made it clear that I was on my own. What changed his mind?

Now, everything was fouled up and I couldn't remain helpless and hidden behind some brush. I knew what I had to do. Bad ankle or not, I used all the strength in my arms to climb over the stone wall. As the rain coated my hair and soaked my clothes I made a run for it, straight to the chimney tower. I could see that the monks were still in the courtyard and the King's men weren't in sight. But I had no idea what I would face once I reached the forge.

Chapter Eighty-three:
Ryn

*T*he heat in the furnace room had become unbearable. Behind me, the two men were down on the floor. The fight had turned vicious with the smaller monk on the receiving end of some nasty well-aimed punches. My eyes were burning from the sweat that was dripping from my forehead, but I got a good look at the bigger guy. Was this the giant that the dark-eyed girl mentioned? He had to be. With the exception of his wild red hair, he could have doubled for the Hulk. But Hulk or not, he and his opponent were inching closer to the flames. One good spark and they'd both be goners.

It's never a good idea to break up a fight. You become the guy in the middle and you get it from both ends. Still, I wasn't about to watch someone go up in flames or melt right in front of my eyes. If I wanted to do that, I could watch *Raiders of the Lost Ark* again. *Think fast, Ryn. Don't just stand there wiping sweat from your eyes. Do something.*

I spun around, bent down and grabbed a fistful of red hair. It wasn't long enough to give it a good yank, but there was enough of it to give the guy a heck of a sting on his head. That was all it took. The man reached for the back of his head and when he did, the guy he was fighting took off. Now, I was the new opponent. *That'll teach you, Ryn, for getting involved.*

When the red-haired guy stood up, I realized that I had made a mistake in judgment. Next to him, the Hulk looked anemic. I had to make a move quickly. A large stack of firewood was a few feet from me, in addition to the pieces that were strewn all over the place when my attacker fell. I got a hold of the biggest, thickest log I could. Then, without stopping to think, I wielded it right into the red-haired guy's knee. Full force. Every bit of energy I could muster. Knee pain is pretty bad. I was counting on it. As the guy winced and reached for his leg, I saw the monk who had just narrowly escaped being burnt to a crisp racing over to the dark-eyed girl. She was still fighting off the other monk who was dragging her to the fire-pit, but this time she had help.

Maybe the guy I managed to release wasn't much of an opponent when it came to exchanging fisticuffs with the red-haired colossus, but he sure was on even ground as he lunged into the man who was all over the dark-eyed girl. It was over in a blink. One solid punch to the man's head and the girl was set free. She watched as her attacker hit his head on the ground and didn't move. Next thing I knew, she threw her arms around the monk who had just delivered the final blow. I felt like yelling, "What about me? What do you think I did?" It was useless. She wouldn't have understood me. All she knew was that some other guy rescued her. I stared as she held tight.

Letting out a slow, deliberate breath, I watched something else. Something I'll never forget. The monk pulled the dark-eyed girl even closer to him and kissed her. And as I stood there watching, I realized something. Linna was watching, too. She had just entered the archway when she saw their lips meet.

Chapter Eighty-four:
Linna

I glanced back at the courtyard as I started to run down the footpath to the forge. The monks were lining up and walking into the church. I couldn't see anyone headed towards me. Thankfully, I didn't see any more of the King's men. Just that first one who was near the wall. I figured he was now in another part of the abbey.

The rain and the wind had formed a steady pattern as I threw my shawl over my head and continued to move quickly. Rain or no rain, the King's men were going to make sure that those monks had that wagon ready. I thought back to that moment when I first saw the man sever the rope under the chassis. I hadn't given it much thought until recently. And then, it occurred to me—I had seen that man. Spoken with him and even ran from him. He was the man who gave me the reliquary box. He knew what those forge monks were hiding under the straw and tried to sabotage them.

And what did I do? I let the forge monks know what had happened by putting the cloth under the wagon. I was to blame, too. I actually helped the wrong faction.

And where was *my* monk in all of this? I hadn't seen him since we were both attacked on the path.

Thoughts of him lying face down on the ground made my stomach tighten as I got closer to the forge. The smoke was so thick that for a moment it was impossible to tell if it was daylight or still night.

That heat! The heat from the furnace was so intense that I could feel it outside the building as I entered the archway. I let my shawl drop to my shoulders as I stepped inside. Just as I looked up, I saw *my* monk and the dark-eyed girl. She flung her arms around him before I could even catch my breath. I stood glued to the spot, unable to process what I was seeing.

I could feel my body tremble as I watched. She clung to him at first and then looked up. He reached his hands to the nape of her neck and moved her closer to him. Slowly, their lips started to meet and his hands moved from her neck to the shoulders, pulling her closer to him. Her arms held tight to his waist and they didn't move. I was numb. And then all of a sudden, the words came flying out of my mouth like bees leaving the hive and I started to run towards them. Worst yet, Ryn was standing directly behind me and he heard everything.

"That was my kiss! That kiss was meant for me, not her. She's stolen my kiss!"

I was livid.

"Thēof ! Who's the thief now?" I screamed.

I was just a few feet from them when I heard Ryn's voice. I couldn't see him clearly in the semi-darkness but his voice was unmistakable.

"Stay put, Linna. Let her have the damn kiss. You want a kiss so bad? Then here!"

At that moment he pulled me close to him and placed both hands on the bottom of my cheeks. Leaning forward, his lips met mine immediately. Then, with an intensity I've never experienced, the pressure on my mouth heightened until I had no choice but to breathe in. I opened my mouth slowly as I fell into his. My voice choked and cracked as I looked straight at him.

"Why did you have to kiss me like that? You've ruined everything!"

"Ruined what? Your fantasy dreams of living with some monk in the Middle Ages? Even Jane Austen wouldn't have gone *that* far!"

"That's not what I meant, Ryn. It's just that…"

And then, as if one kiss wasn't enough, he grabbed me by the shoulders, pulled me close to him and pressed his lips into mine, parting his mouth just slightly. I swore, in that instant, I could feel every part of his being. And the strangest thing was that I didn't care if the dark-eyed girl was kissing *my* monk. In a matter of seconds, none of that mattered.

When I opened my eyes, the green-eyed monk and the girl were no longer in the room. But out of the archways and the alcoves, other monks began to enter. And the only sound I heard was the bellowing of air coming from the furnace.

Chapter Eighty-five:
The Abbey, 1296

*T*he abbot began the Morning Prayer service and looked up as the bell ringer entered the sanctuary. The two men exchanged quick gestures and the abbot understood that some of the monks had been dispensed to the forge. But he knew it would not be enough to stop the *conversi* from carrying out their plans.

As the monks paused for reflection, the abbot cleared his throat and spoke. And when the first words broke from his mouth, he knew he had done the right thing.

"I have kept this a secret for too long, my Brothers. But now we must act. At this very minute, I fear that we have been betrayed. That Scotland has been betrayed. In the forge, some of our Brothers are planning a most heinous deed and we have no recourse but to stop them. It will take all of us to act, not a few."

The abbot took a long, slow breath and continued.

"One by one, we must leave the sanctuary and proceed to the forge. Make haste. Be mindful of the wind and rain, but make haste. Surround the forge so that none may escape. Hold steady your positions.

There are enough of us to form two circles of men around the building. We must go at once."

With that, the abbot placed the small candle from the dais to the table behind him and walked from the altar to the steps that led to the outside cloister. He watched as the monks filed out of the church, their footsteps heavy on the wet ground. Each man paused for just a second to lift the hood over his head. When the abbot finally stepped out of the church, all he could see was a moving tableau of brown heading closer and closer to the forge.

He uttered a silent prayer and then followed behind.

Chapter Eighty-six:
Ryn

~

Linna was holding onto me and shaking. It wasn't exactly the reaction I expected. Then again, I hadn't really thought this out. We were the only ones still standing in the room. The monk and the dark-eyed girl were smart enough to hightail it out of here. The others were still incapacitated on the ground. But never underestimate a thing like that. In all the old horror movies the monsters always manage to spring back up and go for the helpless victim. I took a step back, grabbed Linna's hand and spoke.

"We need to get out of here. Now! Fast!"

Linna just looked at me as if she was seeing me for the first time.

"Oh my God, Ryn! It was you all along! You were the man I thought the King sent. All I could see was the clothing. I had no idea it was you. We were standing so close and I…."

"Yeah, I know. Take it up with Boston Costume. This outfit's going to wind up killing me!"

"But if it was you all along, then the King hasn't sent his men."

"Let's talk about this outside. Come on, Linna. I've got the feeling that something's not right in here. Hurry up! We've got to—"

Before I could finish my sentence, that Goliath of a monk staggered towards me. Only this time he was waving a torch. Somehow he had managed to stand up, get a chunk of firewood and ignite it with one of the oil pots in the room.

"Make a run for it, Linna!" I yelled as I gave her a quick shove towards the archway. I could see the monk inching closer to me, the flames from the torch obscuring his face. My heart was pounding furiously. Linna was already out of the forge, but what I didn't realize was that the monk who had been grappling with the dark-eyed girl had also escaped from the room.

"Don't fight if you can't win! Figure something else out!" I hadn't heard those words in a long time. Seven years maybe. In 1930 Arizona. But all of a sudden, everything snapped into place. I scanned the room like a vulture hawk until I spied one of those oil pots. Then, I raced towards it and heaved it straight at the red-haired monk. And I didn't look back as I ran to the archway.

A few yards from me, that wiry monk who almost succeeded in killing the dark-eyed girl was trying to get a hold of Linna. Apparently, he thought he had another opportunity to finish what he started. But as he grabbed to pull Linna down by the neck, she elbowed him right in the middle of his chest and followed with a sharp kick to one of his ankles. As he started to fall, the rope that was cinched around his waist came loose and with it, a small pouch. Its contents slipped to the ground.

I could hear Linna gasp as she looked down to see what it was—a small piece of parchment paper. And whatever the hell was written on it, it shocked the living daylights out of her.

Chapter Eighty-seven:
The Cottages

The sound of bells clanging and echoing in his ear woke the man from a deep sleep. It was still dark with just a hint of grey on the horizon. The rain had started sometime during the night and continued. The man got up from his cot to check the fire in his hearth, and that's when he noticed that his daughter was not in the cottage.

"Margaretae!" He yelled as he unbolted the door and stepped outside. "Margaretae!"

The bells from the monastery on the hill continued to chime wildly. Loud enough to wake others from their sleep. The man could see that a few of his neighbors had also stepped outside, some holding lanterns. He continued to shout for his daughter.

"Margaretae! Margaretae!"

By now a few of the inhabitants in the small cluster of cottages had started to gather. The man stepped back inside and quickly got dressed. He lit the candle from his lantern and went out to join the others. The crowd had nearly doubled. Never had they heard the abbey bells clang relentlessly. Fearing the worst, the men and boys from the cottages started up the hill.

The wind and rain intensified as the man scanned the berm for his daughter, pausing only now and again to catch his breath. Calling out for her was useless. He hugged the woolen wrap closer to his body and inhaled the scent of boiled yarn. Whatever was amiss at the abbey, he feared that Margaretae was the one in danger.

Wordless, he trudged further up the slope so as not to fall behind the others.

Chapter Eighty-eight:
Linna

I took one look at that piece of parchment and everything I wanted to believe about *my* monk, the green-eyed monk, was a lie. It was the message I had written when I snuck into the small room that the scribes used. I found my monk, all right. I recognized his writing—the formation of his letters—the way in which he stylized everything. But what I failed to recognize was him. My monk, the man I had twisted back time to help, was a killer. And the worst realization of all—the green-eyed monk who had saved me from the bees and had gotten me out of the furnace cellar was not the man I came back in time to save.

And the irony of it all was that I actually succeeded in warning a murderer! I was still holding the parchment when Ryn rushed over to me.

"Are you all right, Linna? Hurry up, that guy isn't going to stay on the ground forever! We've got to get out of here! Quick! There's a wooded area right in front of us!"

"That's where the wagon is, Ryn. And the reason those forge monks wanted to kill me, well…kill the girl they thought was me. It's about what's in that wagon. I didn't figure out the whole thing until just now."

"Great, Linna. Keep running."

"But…."

Straight ahead, I saw them—the girl who looked like me and the monk I thought was mine. They were hunched over the wagon, throwing the large pieces of metal as far as they could down the hill.

"Ryn, that wagon is full of weapons. That's what those monks were smelting. They've been supplying arms to someone and I figured out who. I've heard them talk. They've used the word *Angelcyning*. It's Old English for *English King—The King of England*. Right now they're ruled by a Scottish king. But it looks like this monastery was tricked into helping start a war."

"Evidently, I'm the new poster child for it! That must explain why those monks locked me in the bell tower. When I get back, I will personally present a lawsuit to Boston Costume! Boy, can you pick a time and place, Linna! We've really got to get out of here!"

Next thing I knew, he grabbed my hand and gave it a quick pull.

"Hurry up; we've got to make it down this—"

He had stopped speaking. Long enough for me to take in what he had already seen. I gasped on my own words.

"Oh my God. The whole village down there is headed this way. And they're against the King, too!"

"Terrific! Just duck down under the bushes by these trees. We'll wait it out and then make a run for it."

I got down on my knees and moved in closer to Ryn. Off to our right, I could see the green-eyed monk and the girl still throwing pieces of metal. He had no idea that the girl he had kissed in the forge wasn't me. And apparently, neither did the other scribe who tried to kill her. I managed to fight him off, but I had the gut wrenching feeling that he'd get up any minute to finish what he started.

Chapter Eighty-nine:
The Abbey, 1296

The rain had started to slow and the wind began to die down as the monks gradually took their places around the forge. The *conversi* who had entered from the passageways below had no idea that the building was being surrounded. They tried to make sense of the screaming red-haired monk who was covered in oil and stumbling about the room waving his torch.

A few of the men tried to restrain him, only to be kicked and threatened. Others immediately tended to the fire and salvaged what little ore had remained. They moved quickly. It was well past dawn.

Screaming uncontrollably, Brother Rulf raced out of the forge. The rain had washed some of the thick oil from his face as he stood in the archway taking in the scene that was in front of him. All of the monks from the abbey were lined up twofold around the building. He estimated at least forty of them and they weren't about to move. Running back inside the forge, he yelled for the men to head down the passageway, but it was too late. Someone had bolted the wooden doors from the other side.

The heat in the room had risen to an unbearable level. The men ignored the red-haired monk and made their way out of the building. But there was no place they could go. The entire order of monks stood silently in front of them. No one could have anticipated what was about to happen.

With all the fury and anger that had been pent up inside of him, Brother Rulf tore through the crowd and ran towards the spot where the wagon was kept, using the flames from his torch to keep everyone away.

Straight ahead of him he could see Brother Gregory and the girl, throwing the last of the weapons down the berm. He moved closer, his voice bellowing. Just as he reached the edge of the wooded area, someone came out from behind him, grabbed his hood, and pulled him to the ground. The torch rolled a few feet and then sizzled and spurted as the rain-drenched ground extinguished the fire.

"It is over, my brother. We have failed King Edward and we have failed ourselves."

The red-haired monk turned to see his younger brother reaching out his hand.

"The Abbey, I fear, will not take kindly to us."

As Brother Rulf stood up, the circle of monks moved forward until it engulfed him. The silence was more powerful than any storm he had ever witnessed. And the rain slowly released its grip on the abbey, letting in a faint beam of sunlight.

Chapter Ninety:
Ryn

I glanced over my shoulder to the hill below us. Mary Shelley couldn't have staged it better if she tried. It was a scene straight out of *Frankenstein*. The people from the cottages below were coming up the slope. Only they were carrying lanterns, not torches. But still, I half expected them to chant, *"We've come for the monster."* The villagers always come for the monster. Only this time, I knew they were coming for me.

That dark-eyed girl must have told her father that she sent one of the English King's men to the abbey. Then, all those bells started clanging. Enough to wake an entire campus after a Friday night football game. Of course they were coming for me. Terrific. I was trapped from both ends.

Just then we heard a rustling a few feet from us. Linna pressed herself against me and grabbed my wrist.

"It's okay," I whispered. "Stay still."

The red-haired monk had made his way towards the wagon, but the scribe who had fought with Linna managed to topple the guy to the ground. We held our breath and watched. Slowly, a line of monks surrounded them. Behind us, the green-eyed monk and the girl must have been watching, too. But none of us dared to make a move.

Linna turned her head towards mine as she spoke.

"Do you think we can get out of here, Ryn?"

"With about as much chance as Butch Cassidy and the Sundance Kid."

Her face turned pale and she just stared.

"Hold on, Linna. We don't need to get *out*, we need to get *back*. I still have the prism and the sun is just coming out."

"What about the vibrations? Without them, we'll only travel in time, not space."

I was about to answer her when suddenly I could hear someone else speaking. Loudly. Clearly. But in a language I didn't understand.

Chapter Ninety-one: The Abbey, 1296

The silence was deafening as the circle of monks drew tighter. They were closing in on the red-haired monk and the scribe. No one knew that the man they presumed to be the English King's messenger was carefully hidden in the small clump of brush underneath the trees. And with him, a girl who resembled another from one of the cottages below.

As the monks drew closer to their two Brothers, a third figure appeared and broke through the circle. He looked worn and tired but with a steady resolve. When he had reached the spot where the men were standing, he stretched out his arms and spoke.

"As abbot of this monastery I must ensure that our abbey remains a place of service and worship to God. I have been remiss in not recognizing the evil that started to grow within our cloister walls, and for that, I shall give penance. With a heart burdened by sorrow, I must now dismiss two of our Brothers. Though they pose as men of the cloth, they are not. They have deceived and beguiled us. Are they murderers in our midst? That is

for God alone to determine. But hear this—Brother Rulf and Brother Dain, you are to leave the abbey at once."

Then, turning to the forge monks who stood by the archway, the abbot continued to speak.

"We cannot and will not have two orders within our walls. Those of you who wish to leave and serve in the secular world, I bid you well. And for those who wish to remain, you shall do so with a free and clear conscience."

A few of the *conversi* nodded and stepped out of the circle. They walked towards the red-haired monk and his brother without saying a word. The defeated cluster of men took the footpath from the forge to the church and proceeded down the hill, barely acknowledging the villagers who were only a few yards away.

In the faint sunlight, the men and boys from the cottages gradually blew out the candles in their lanterns and continued up the slope past the apiary until they reached the edge of the cloister. They could see the gathering of monks near the forge.

All of a sudden, one of the men started to run towards the chimney tower. His voice echoed off the cloister walls.

"Margaretae! Margaretae!"

The man moved closer. Still calling for his daughter.

Slowly, from behind the woods, came a green-eyed monk holding the girl's hand.

Chapter Ninety-two:
Linna

Everything seemed to happen in slow motion—the fighting, the circle of monks and the people from the village walking up the hill. I was leaning so close to Ryn that I could actually feel his heart beating. I knew it was time for us to leave. *My* monk never really existed. Not the one I envisioned anyway. And the green-eyed monk… well, he wasn't mine either. Yet something inexplicable drew me to this place and time. It wasn't until much later that I understood.

Ryn leaned over and nudged my shoulder.

"Take a good look. The abbot is banishing those monks. Once everyone leaves, we might have a decent chance of getting out of here ourselves. That is if the villagers don't get to us first."

I took a deep breath and waited. It was like watching someone else's dream. Until the very instant when I heard a man scream.

"Margaretae! Margaretae!"

The the next thing I knew he was running straight past the chimney tower to the archway in front of the forge. The monks were still surrounding the building but their circle had loosened. Enough to let the man through until he was face to face with the abbot.

"Margaretae!"

I watched as the abbot pointed to the area where the wagon was kept. The girl who looked like me was running toward her father and alongside of her was the green-eyed monk.

"You're not going to get all sappy and crazy over this are you?" Ryn whispered. "Because if you are, I swear I'm going to kiss you again!"

"If that's what it takes, I will."

"Shh… watch what's happening."

All I could see was the green-eyed monk talking with the abbot. The man placed his hands on the monk's shoulders and nodded. The girl hugged her father and the four of them walked past the forge down the walkway to the church. Behind them, the monks lined up and followed. Then, the man turned and said something to the people from the cottages, because they, too, started to follow the procession towards the church.

"We can stand up now," Ryn said. "They're all gone." And just as I started to brush off the dirt from my clothing, I heard the pealing of bells.

Chapter Ninety-three:
Ryn

Maybe I was delusional but it seemed as if Linna had miraculously gotten over her fantasy love affair with that monk. Did that mean we had a decent chance of resuming the relationship we started back in high school? I didn't know. The only thing that mattered at that moment was getting the heck out of here and back to our own time.

Any chance at all of using the vibration from the bells was gone. They only rang for a few minutes. I looked at Linna and could see that she was getting nervous. I grabbed her hand and spoke.

"Hey, the worst thing that will happen is that we wind up in Scotland in our time."

"With no passports, no money and these awful outfits."

"Actually, Aeden and I have been through worse."

In that instant, I had a thought. Not the best scenario, but one that might work.

"Linna! The bees! Those hives are just below us at the edge of the woods. All we need to do is set them off and they'll start buzzing. Buzzing! Vibrations! We can figure this out!"

"If we don't get stung to death first."

"We don't have another choice. Let's go!"

The sun was playing tag with the remaining clouds as we got closer to the apiary. Not a good thing when a beam of direct light is needed for time travel. I knew what would happen if the beam was too narrow for both of us. One of us would get stuck in this time and place or worse yet, slip into another. I just kept hoping the clouds would disappear.

The beehives were quiet when we approached. I don't know why but I expected at least a few of those guys to be buzzing and swarming about. Then, I remembered something from a biology class a long time ago—bees are only active when they are warm. Hell. It had been raining most of the night and the sun wasn't strong enough yet. I just hoped Linna wouldn't get unglued the way Aeden did when things went berserk.

"Linna, we've got to wait this out for a few minutes. Maybe longer. The sun has to start heating up the hives."

"Can't we just throw something at them?"

I shook my head.

"That's not the problem. There isn't enough sunlight."

"Oh my God, Ryn. You're right. Worse yet, I don't think we have a whole lot of time. See for yourself!"

I looked down the hill to where Linna was pointing and saw what appeared to be men on horseback. But not just any men. These men were wearing armor and carrying lances.

"King Edward's men?" Linna asked. "Or King John's?"

"Does it really matter? We don't have a choice. Grab some rocks and start throwing them at the hives."

It only took a few seconds, but it seemed like hours until the bees started swarming. It wasn't as steady or direct as using an electric toothbrush, but it was better than nothing. I just had no idea where we'd really wind up. Not to mention the matter of "entry." Linna and I had both entered the time-space continuum from different points in time. Did that mean we were going to end up months apart?

I wasn't up for the "Physicist of the Year" award. I just wanted to get us the hell out. Whichever king was sending his army, those guys were already halfway up the hill.

My hand was pretty steady considering that we were surrounded by bees. The edge of the prism captured the sunlight just as I grabbed Linna and held her tight with one hand around her waist. The last thing I remembered was getting stung on the neck. I winced and we both moved a few steps back. Then… nothing.

Chapter Ninety-four: Linna

My neck rested on the base of Ryn's shoulder as he pulled me closer to him. I could feel his arm around my waist and I put both of my arms around his. Then, for just a second he stumbled back and I almost toppled over him. By then, it was too late. Time had taken us, but I had no idea where or when.

Unlike the first time, my head began to hurt and it felt as if my entire body was spinning out of control. There was no way I could open my eyes, and even if I could, I was too petrified to try. There were moments when I thought I was still clinging to Ryn and then there were horrific seconds when it was as if I was flying wildly in space with no way back. And the strangest part of it all was the fact that I didn't even know if I was breathing.

Suddenly my body began to feel as if there was a tremendous weight on it. I was no longer whirling in time and space. I could feel a cold hard surface underneath me, but I couldn't move. My head began to clear, but I was still too scared to open my eyes. It was only when the weight seemed to lift and I heard Ryn's voice that I dared to look.

"Take a deep breath, Linna. You're okay. I must have fallen and pushed all the air out of your lungs when we clicked back in time."

I opened my eyes slowly. Everything was blurry, but I recognized the room. It was the small study in my apartment. For some reason I couldn't get my voice above a whisper but I tried.

"Ryn, we're in Georgetown. My apartment."

"Just take deep breaths. Slow down."

I spoke again. This time it was audible.

"We made it back. Oh my God. We made it back."

Ryn held out his hand and I steadied myself as I stood up.

"This is unbelievable. The room still looks the same."

"The same as when, Linna? Take your time."

My vision was coming back and I walked over to my desk. My iPhone was on top of the parchment roll that I had been translating. And the last number entered was Ryn's.

"We came back a few days before I left and weeks before you did. This is the night I called you. That first night. When I asked you to help me go back in time."

"Oh no. No. No. No."

"It's not that bad is it? We haven't lost any time at all. We've gained time."

"Yeah. Terrific. It means I've got to get a flight to Boston and take my finals all over again!"

I smiled and shrugged my shoulders.

"What do you want to do first? Book a flight or go out and get some clothes?"

"You forgot the third option."

"What's that?"

And then Ryn stepped towards me and placed his hands on my elbows, moving me closer to him. His arms gently grazed mine as they slowly reached my shoulders and neck. I leaned in as my lips met his. It was the longest, sweetest kiss I could ever imagine. And I knew at that moment it wasn't a monk I was in love with, it was a time borrower.

Chapter Ninety-five:
Ryn

It was Columbus Day weekend and Linna had managed to catch a flight into Boston for a few days. It was the first time we had seen each other since that night in Georgetown. Sprawling on the couch in my living room, it felt as if that entire Scotland nightmare was just that—a dream. Time travel does that to you. It's real the moment you experience it but once you return to your own place in time it becomes faded and blurry. Only the sensations and emotions remain solid.

As Linna leaned against me, I thought about why she was so driven to go back in time for that monk. It wasn't a jealous thing. Just a nagging feeling that there was more to it. Like the time Aeden and I wound up having to save our bloodline during the French Revolution. And all of sudden, everything became clear.

"Linna!" I said, startling her from the cozy position she had lying next to me. "Remember back in eighth grade when we were doing those ancestry projects for Social Studies?"

Before she had a chance to catch her breath, I continued.

"Well, I remember yours. Your family came to the United States from Ireland. You put down 'Irish' for your background, but it was really Scottish. I remember you trying to tell the teacher that your father's family was called 'Ulster Scots.' But since they emigrated from Ireland, your ancestry was listed as Irish."

"Ryn, you don't suppose—"

"I do. That girl…the one that looked just like you…she had to have been your ancestor. In fact, put her and that monk together and guess what Linna? I think that was the start of your bloodline!"

"Ew…this is getting creepy. I was actually holding his hand."

"Oh big deal. Everyone holds hands. Don't you get it? If you didn't go back in time, he would never have met her. Margaretae! That was her name. You had to be drawn back in time in order to ensure that your family line began."

"This is much too weird for me to comprehend, Ryn."

"It always is."

Just then, my phone buzzed and I looked at the text. Aeden!

"U 2 up 4 pizza?"

Linna could see the expression on my face.

"You haven't told her, have you? I mean about you going back in time?"

"Actually, I did. But it never happened and she won't believe me."

"So now what?"

"Now, I face the worst punishment ever. This spring her college will be presenting *Macbeth*. And I'll be forced to sit through every single performance!"

THE END

Epilogue

Gregory of Scryngeour and Margaretae Sules were married by the abbot at sunset on the day that Linna Sullivan returned to the 21st century. On that same day, brothers Rulf and Dain pledged allegiance to King Edward I when they encountered his horsemen on the hill to the monastery.

But as fate would have it, the horsemen approached the apiary too closely and the bees swarmed relentlessly, forcing the men back down the hill. They returned weeks later with reinforcements to seize the abbey from the monks. By that time, the quiet and peaceful men of the cloth had shuttered the structures and had taken refuge in other monastic dwellings before finally settling at the Pluscarden Abbey to the north, in Moray.

The Monastery in East Lothian was destroyed during the First War of Scottish Independence. It never saw the 14th century. But the parchments and codices that its scribes labored to produce were hidden inside the passageways beneath the cloisters. They were discovered in the early 21st century and made their way into universities in Edinburgh, London, Paris, and Washington, D.C.

Endnotes

In 1292, John Balliol, the son of a Scottish lord, was appointed King of Scotland, following an intense arbitration in which King Edward I of England served as judge. Some scholars hold that King Edward I wished to have a "puppet" sitting on Scotland's throne. The caveat was clear—John Balliol had to swear loyalty to England's King. And he did.

Three years later, John Balliol signed a treaty with France, signaling an alliance with their King, Phillip IV. France was England's enemy and Edward I would not tolerate this betrayal. He retaliated against Scotland with a military invasion that prompted the first conflict in a series of wars for Scottish independence. The Battle of Dunbar gave England its victory.

Ultimately, Edward I conquered Scotland and John Balliol was forced to abdicate the throne.

Works Cited for
The Time Borrower

http://en.wikipedia.org/wiki/Blast_furnace

http://en.wikipedia.org/wiki/Vibration

http://justus.anglican.org/resources/bcp/Scotland/james
6_notes.html

http://saburchill.com/history/chapters/chap5102.html

www.bbc.co.uk/scotland/history/articles/edward_i/

www.britroyals.com

www.dwalker.pwp.blueyonder.co.uk

www.educationscotland.gov.uk/higherscottishhistory/w
arsofindependence/index.asp

www.internationalschooltoulouse.net/vs/pilgrims/relics.
htm

www.middle-ages.org.uk/daily-life-monk-middle-
ages.htm

www.militaryhistory.about.com/od/battleswars1201140
0/p/dunbar12...

www.mittelzeit.blogspot.com

www.oldenglishtranslator.co.uk

www.pluscardenabbey.org/home.asp

www.shakespeareandhistory.com/john-baliol-king-of-
scotland.php

Study Guide for
The Time Borrower

This young adult novel blends historical and science fiction. The study guide component provides teachers with differentiated questions and activities designed to develop thinking skills and promote a better understanding of this particular era in time. The study guide is reproducible for classroom use.

Chapters One — Five:

1. What is a liturgy?
2. What is Ryn's initial reaction to Linna's call? Would you have felt the same way?
3. Why is Linna so driven to get Ryn's help?
4. If you were Ryn, would you have shared your formulas? Explain your reasoning.
5. What obstacles does Ryn believe Linna will encounter? Explain.
6. Why do you suppose that Ryn doesn't want to tell his sister about incorporating vibrations into their formulas for time travel?

Chapters Six — Ten:

1. Linna equates the vibrations surrounding her body with a ceiling fan. Can you come up with other examples? List at least two.
2. What are Matins prayers?
3. What is a refractory?
4. What did Linna mean when she said, "There was more to fear in the little cottage than ghosts?"
5. What do you think the monks were carving in the wine cellar?
6. How did the monks communicate without speaking?

Chapters Eleven — Fifteen:

1. What is a Compline service?
2. Describe Brother Gregory's fear. Have you ever been that afraid? Explain.
3. How would you describe Linna's actions regarding food and sleep? Would you have taken the same chances? Why or why not?
4. What is the irony regarding Linna's footsteps in the snow?
5. If you were Ryn's sister, would you have told him about Linna's actions when she was in his room alone?
6. What is the formula for Snell's Law?

Chapters Sixteen — Twenty:

1. What do you think Linna found in that box?
2. How do you think Linna figured out the words *"Later, after dark."*
3. See if you can write a paragraph or a short poem with an encrypted text.
4. Why does Linna think that the monk who saved her from the bees is the one she came back in time to help?
5. Have you ever been "thunderstruck?" Explain.

Chapters Twenty-one — Twenty-five:

1. What is a precentor? What role does he play in an abbey?
2. Yes or no. The young monk has mixed feelings about Linna.
3. What does Linna discover about the monastery?
4. Do you believe that Shakespeare's *Macbeth* is indeed a "cursed" play? (You may want to do a bit of research before you answer.)
5. What do you think Linna sees in the wagon?

Chapters Twenty-six — Thirty:

1. Describe Brother Rulf.
2. How would you communicate with someone who didn't speak your language?

3. Was your original prediction about the contents of the box correct?
4. What is a reliquary? Why were they so valued and why would anyone create forgeries?
5. Who do you suppose the other girl is?
6. How does Linna know that the reliquary is a fake? Explain your reasoning.

Chapters Thirty-one — Thirty- five:

1. If you were Linna, would you have gone back up the hill to the abbey or followed the girl? Explain.
2. What are *conversi* monks?
3. Why is Brother Gregory conflicted?
4. Even if you don't understand Latin, using what you do know about the English language, try to translate the sentence *"De monasterio exire! Non es securus."*
5. Yes or no. Linna still cares about Ryn. Support your answer.
6. Why did Brother Rulf chase Linna down the hill?

Chapters Thirty-six — Forty:

1. What was the scribe's reaction to Linna's warning?
2. What is a triumvirate?

3. What are Kabbalistic prayers?
4. What would you do if you received Charlotte Campbell's message? What do you think Ryn will do?
5. What did Brother Gregory mean when he said that the girl *"had more to fear than just bees?"*
6. List at least four different types of monks that were prevalent during the Middle Ages.
7. Yes or no. Ryn has a viable plan to get Linna back to the 21st century. If you answered no, what plan would you create?

Chapters Forty-one — Forty-five:

1. Do you think "the end justifies the means" regarding the actions that Brothers Alban and Trewyn took to fund the monastery? Can you think of examples in history where deceit was used to obtain a greater good. Do you agree?
2. Brother Gregory does not tell anyone about his gruesome discovery in the forge. Do you agree with his actions? Why or why not?
3. Who is "Monty Python?" Can you name any of their movies? (Give yourself a star if you've seen any of these movies!)
4. What is the consequence for adding vibrations to Snell's Law?

5. Why do you suppose it took Brother Gregory so long to figure out that Linna was in the cellar under the forge?
6. Who wrote *Canterbury Tales?* *Add it to your reading list before you graduate from high school!
7. Who do the monks think Ryn is? Why?

Chapters Forty-six — Fifty:

1. Do you think the monk will return to the cellar to save Linna? Explain.
2. What became of Brother Alban?
3. Why do you think the dark-eyed girl helped Ryn? Or, do you think she was setting a trap? Explain.

Chapters Fifty-one — Fifty-five:

1. What do you think the abbot intends to do with "King Edward's man?"
2. Think of three words (or more) that would describe how Linna felt about the monk who rescued her.
3. Re-write any three sentences from the dialogue into the modern English that we speak today.
4. Why do you suppose the scribe went back for more of the poisoned potion? Couldn't he have just killed Linna?

5. Charlotte Campbell cancelled her date because she was so mesmerized by what she was translating. Have you ever done something that was so fascinating that you cancelled dates and appointments, too? Explain.

Chapters Fifty-six — Sixty:

1. What would you do if you were in Ryn's predicament in the bell tower?
2. The scribe has a conscience. Yes or no.
3. How does the dark-eyed girl's conscience plague her?
4. Find Edinburgh and Dunbar on a map of Scotland.
5. Is Ryn brave or reckless? Explain.

Chapters Sixty-one — Sixty-five:

1. Why do you suppose Brother Gregory did not recognize who his attacker was?
2. What's a belfry?
3. How does Ryn figure out how to get down from the tower?
4. What kind of man is Brother Rulf? Justify your answer with examples from the text.
5. If you could give Linna advice, what would you tell her?

Chapters Sixty-six — Seventy:

1. Was the dark-eyed girl the intended victim for the man who tripped her? Explain.
2. Ryn talks about an "automatic zone." Can you explain what he means? Has this ever happened to you?
3. What spiritual "battle" is Brother Gregory facing?
4. What ultimately saved Ryn from his death?

Chapters Seventy-one — Seventy-five:

1. What is an Angelus Bell?
2. Who was Ryn really chasing?
3. Why does Linna mistake Ryn for someone else?

Chapters Seventy-six — Eighty:

1. Yes or no. Ryn is really "over" Linna. Have you ever felt that way about someone?
2. Why does the abbot feel guilty? Explain.
3. Ryn, who is thought to be the "King's man," witnesses two gruesome scenes in the forge. If you were Ryn, what would you have done?
4. Ryn compares the King's men to cockroaches and ants. What other comparisons can you make?

Chapters Eighty-one — Eighty-five:

1. What is a ruse? What was the ruse that Brother Rulf perpetuated?
2. Why do you think Linna was brought back in time?
3. Ryn says that, "It's never a good idea to break up a fight." Do you agree or disagree? Explain.
4. Do you think it was "the kiss" that made Linna realize how she felt about Ryn, or was she hiding her feelings all along? Use examples from the text to support your reasoning.
5. Do you think the abbot can stop the *conversi* from committing the deed they had planned?

Chapters Eighty-six — Ninety:

1. Do you agree with Ryn's philosophy *Don't Fight If You Can't Win?* Explain.
2. Who is Margaretae?
3. What truth does Linna uncover about her actions?
4. Who is Brother Rulf's actual brother?
5. Who is Mary Shelley? Do you know who her husband was? Better yet, have you read any of his poetry? (Give yourself a double star if you answered yes to these questions. If not, it's a good time to find a search engine!)

Chapters Ninety-one — Ninety-five:

1. Why doesn't the abbot want to continue having two distinct "orders" in the abbey? Explain.
2. What do you think the green-eyed monk and Margaretae will do next?
3. Explain the matter of "entry" when it comes to the time-space continuum.
4. Where did you expect Ryn and Linna to wind up in time?
5. Should Ryn tell his sister, Aeden, the truth? If you were Aeden, how would you react?

Bonus Question: Who was the "time borrower?" Explain your reasoning.

Theoretical Questions

1. How is a monastery like a beehive? Give at least three examples.
2. Can you think of another simile for the monastery?
3. Find examples of figurative language in this novel. (i.e., metaphor, simile, allusion, alliteration, onomatopoeia, hyperbole, personification, cliché).

4. Do you think an organization like the Monastery at Lothian can survive with two separate orders or tiers? Can you give examples of organizations where this is practiced?

Thematic Projects

1. Make a scale drawing of a 13th-century monastery in Scotland or England.
2. Construct a three-dimensional 13th-century blast furnace. (Visual version only!)
3. Find images of reliquaries via a computer search.
4. Draw a hierarchy of monks and their duties. (It will differ according to their order and monastery.)
5. Research Edward I and John Balliol.
6. Compare the Scottish Wars of Independence with the American War of Independence (Revolutionary War).

Acknowledgements

How I transfer the thoughts in my mind to the screen in front of me is such an enigma. What I see clearly may turn out to be jumbled and blurry for the reader. If it wasn't for my publisher (Two Cats Press) and my amazing team of editors and proofreaders, none of this would be possible. From logistics and continuity, to form and function, they hold me accountable. I am forever in their debt.

Thank you, Ellen Lynes, Susan Morrow, Suzanne Scher, Susan Schwartz, Steve Somers, and Lisa Tonks.

And a special thank you to my husband, James Clapp, for supporting me every step of the way. I promise, I'll cook dinner sometime!

About the Author

New York native Ann I. Goldfarb spent most of her life in education, first as a classroom teacher and later as a middle school principal and professional staff developer. Writing has always been an integral part of her world. For the past decade, she has written non-fiction for Madavor Media/Jones Publishing, but her real passion is writing mystery-suspense-adventure for young adult audiences. Time travel, the vehicle she embraces, is her hook into historical fiction.

The Face Out of Time received a literary award from Arizona Authors Association in 2011 and her novels, *The Last Tag* and *Light Riders and the Morenci Mine Murder,* were finalists in the 2012 and 2013 New Mexico-Arizona Book Awards respectively. *Light Riders and the Morenci Mine Murder* took second place in the 2013 Purple Dragonfly Book Awards for excellence in children's and YA fiction.

Ann resides with her family near the foothills of the White Tank Mountains in Arizona. She invites you to visit her website at www.timetravelmysteries.com and "LIKE" her Facebook Page—Time Travel Mysteries.

www.ingramcontent.com/pod-product-compliance
Lightning Source LLC
Chambersburg PA
CBHW051253210726

48287CB00002B/477